THE
WOMAN
WHO
MARRIED
A BEAR

THE
WOMAN
WHO
MARRIED
A BEAR

JOHN STRALEY

VICTOR GOLLANCZ
LONDON

First published in Great Britain 1995
by Victor Gollancz
An imprint of the Cassell Group
Wellington House, 125 Strand, London WC2R 0BB

First published in the United States 1992
by Soho Press, New York

A catalogue record for this book is
available from the British Library

ISBN 0 575 06027 1

Printed in Great Britain by
St Edmundsbury Press Ltd, Bury St Edmunds, Suffolk

AUTHOR'S NOTE

In 1984, when I was starting out as a private investigator, a Tlingit woman told me about a woman who had married a bear and had children by him. She swore it was true, and I believed her.

There are many stories about the coupling of bears and human beings. These stories appear in languages throughout the north. The version that I was told differs from other versions collected by scholars and folklorists. The seed that eventually became this book may have been a combination of two traditional stories, one about a man who married a bear and the other of a woman. One is a coastal story from southeastern Alaska and the other comes from the northern interior. This novel is not meant to displace or contradict any of the scholarly work that has been done by such people as Dick and Nora Dauenhauer, and Catherine McClellan, Gary Snyder or Paul Shepard. It is also not meant to displace the vibrant stories that are still being told in kitchens and around fires all over the north.

The characters and events of this story are products of my labor and imagination. Alaska, of course, remains very real. The cities of Sitka, Juneau, and Anchorage are easily found on current maps. The town of Stellar is fictional.

This book could not have reached this form without a great deal of help. In many ways, both obvious and obscure, it is a collaborative work, and I want to express my most grateful thanks to the people who helped it along its way: To Nita Couchman, Lauren Davis, Ann Douglas, Rick Friedman, Galen Paine, Jake Schumacher, Jan Straley, and Robin Viens for reviewing the manuscript in its various stages and saving me from the more obvious forms of embarrassment.

To Juris Jurjevics and Laura Hruska of Soho Press for pulling me off the pile, and breathing some life into my work.

And to my friends and teachers, Annie Jacobs, Joseph Moriarity and Nelson Bentley, for their generosity and their love of words: written, spoken, and sung.

For Walter Straley
who taught me everything, by example.

THE
WOMAN
WHO
MARRIED
A BEAR

ONE

> My head is a cup left out
> on a stormy autumn night;
> half full of water, and a spider.

I had botched my seventeen syllables, my money was gone, and my only credit card was missing. The worst of it was I didn't remember if it was stolen or given away. I sat on the green bench in front of the Pioneer Home with my wallet sitting in my hand, as useless as a ticket for a ferry I had just missed. I felt like I had a spider digging into my inner ear, and a fur-bearing animal trying to claw its way out of my stomach. This was the beginning of an extraordinarily bad day. Even if it wasn't raining.

I've tried other hangover cures besides haiku. Once, I had grabbed the back of the radio that was chained to the bed of my hotel room in Rock Springs, Wyoming, hoping, as the voice said, that "the blessed power of Jesus" would fill my soul. Besides a brief jolt of 110—nothing. I've tried

3

reading poetry in hopes that the sludge of alcohol would
melt into the atmosphere. This morning I had found a book
by Wendell Berry flopping in the bottom of my bed like a
cold hot-water bottle. The woman who used to love me left it
on my bedside table before leaving me. I had thrown it in my
pocket before going out. Tempting fate. But no jolt of clarity
came; I never got past the inscription. In green ink she had
written, "There is nowhere to stand but in absence, no life
but in the fateful light." She was cute, and now a Christian.
Her skin was as white as a sea anemone, and as soft as the
pool of warm air you pass through while rowing across the
bay. I didn't know why in the hell she had written that.

Once, I'd thought that I could cure a hangover by swimming in the cold water off my house. I'd eased my body into
the Pacific Ocean that joins the Gulf of Alaska just past the
channel: numbness, and needles of pain, like remembering
and forgetting all at once. Going into the ocean, my feet, my
legs, my testicles; it seemed like such a tight fit.

I broke off a piece of bread from a two-day-old sandwich
that was tucked into my windbreaker and flipped it onto the
cement sidewalk. The raven watching me dropped into a
crowd of plump pigeons and snatched it away. A large black
bird with a gently curving beak, he sat on the back of my
bench, cackling like a fiend. I looked at him carefully and
noticed he had a loop of red thread hooked around his left
leg. Maybe someone had tried to snare him: a kid with a long
stick and a mound of bait, waiting, waiting for the bird to
drop and then losing him as soon as the slack was pulled.
Raven the trickster: the missing piece of darkness.

The Pioneer Home is an old folks' home run by the state
of Alaska. I had an appointment to see one of the residents
but I was sitting outside killing time while they carefully

made their way around their breakfast. I thought of their bran cereal and coffee. I thought of the brass ship's clock that ticks loudly and unheard in the corner. I had about ten minutes.

I flipped a piece of cheese to the raven and tried to run down last night's events. I remembered bumping into Wynton Duarte. Wynton is an unsuccessful drug dealer and decent storyteller, but yesterday he was taking and not giving. There is a parity that must be maintained with people who tell stories for a living and Wynton had wanted to know the story about a particular police informant who was rumored to be in town.

The home looks like a stately old seaside hotel. It's bordered by flower gardens and lawns that sit in the middle of town across from the post office. The post office is the center of the community where most of the eight thousand people in Sitka still come to pick up their mail. Next to it is the hill where the official transfer of Alaska from Russia to the United States took place and where Alexander Baranof, the manager of the Russian American Company, built his first leaky-roofed cabin. A stone wall borders the lawns of the home. It runs at waist height along the two main streets that meet in the corner at the center of town. Katlian is named for the Tlingit warrior who almost whipped the Russian thugs with a blacksmith's hammer, the other is named for Abraham Lincoln.

It's on this wall that many of Sitka's pink-cheeked youths, including Wynton Duarte, sit and drink rum and smoke reefer, plotting their many small and unobtrusive crimes. When a tour ship comes in to dump hundreds of rain-jacketed, camera-laden tourists, the youths are encouraged by the friendly small-town police officers to recreate elsewhere. Often, they will move their parties up into one of the deserted Russian cemeteries, drinking rum and listening to chainsaw guitar riffs from their tape players. They sit on the overturned gravestones in the dense forest, their music drifting into town like the sound of machinery from a clearcut.

I'd been drinking for a while, maybe days, but last night I'd found myself with Duarte and some guys off a black cod boat sitting on the wall drinking apple wine mixed with grain alcohol, and after several drinks it occurred to someone that we all should go to a restaurant and eat some pizza and drink some Mexican beer that I could charge on my credit card. Of the rest of the evening I have mostly an impressionistic collage. Floating in the foreground is a leather-clad singer who reminded me of Marlene Dietrich in *The Blue Angel,* her tone searing through the fog, like the whine of an outboard. I remember the fo'c'sle of a halibut schooner, tequila, a woman changing her shirt and talking about a horse in Montana, someone crying and some vague talk about a gun.

When I woke up, in my own bed, there was blood on my sleeve. From the feel of my nose, the blood might have been mine. Duarte, my money and my charge card were among the missing. I listened to a message on my answering machine telling me to come to the Pioneer Home to speak to Mrs. Victor. I could tell as she spoke that she was serious. There was a percussive melody in her voice as if she had learned to speak from the raven. She was insistent: I needed to speak to her this morning.

I heard people shuffling out of the dining hall in the home. I shook the crumbs out of my pocket and then jammed the last part of the sandwich back in. There was a woman in peach-colored slacks standing in the middle of the street trying to watch for traffic and take a picture of the Russian Orthodox Cathedral at the same time. This involved a lot of head bobbing and hand waving from her husband on the sidewalk. A raven was the only one sitting on the wall now. A slight breeze off the harbor ruffled his feathers, and as he watched he made noises deep in his throat that sounded like stones dropping into a well.

The tourist lady fussed with her hair and looked nervously up and down the street, even though there were no cars in sight this Sunday morning. She snapped the shot, scurried to her husband, and the raven flew to the curb in front of a bar where he began to eat what looked like the remnants of a pickled egg.

I walked up the steps of the home and in through the double doors. I had left the book by Wendell Berry on the bench outside. No one steals books, and poetry is particularly safe. It would be there when I came out.

When you think of a state-run institution for the aged, you might imagine hollow eyes behind a web of shadows. Emptiness, desperation. In this way the home is a disappointment. To be sure, there are people sitting around, but most of them are waiting to start an argument about fish and game regulations or how the state should spend the oil money to establish craft guilds or senior citizens' advisory boards. The place is well lit and the halls have thick carpet to avoid the executioner's sound of nurses' shoes squeaking on linoleum.

I looked up Mrs. Victor's room number on the front board in the lobby and I walked down the first-floor hall to room 104. Behind one door there was florid organ music from a TV and a woman's voice with a Boston accent saying, "I

don't have to stand here and be made a fool of, Gregory!"
Then music swells and the commercial break. Then a
human voice: "Come on, drink it and I'll ask the doctor
about new medication when he comes by."

I expected Mrs. Victor's room to be tomblike. Dark and
small, with the smell of medicine and cleaning products. I
knocked and heard a faint rustling behind the door. When I
opened it I stepped into a searing light. The sun was coming
up through her open window and all of her lamps were lit.
She sat in the corner, sunk down in her wheelchair, elbows
propped out like chicken wings on the armrests. She was
smoking a cigarette, and the ticking of the clock in her room
was unusually loud as if time had just begun.

"Mrs. Victor? I'm Cecil Younger. Did you want to see
me?" I took off my leather windbreaker and draped it over
my arm. "Mrs. Victor?" I had to shade my eyes to face her.

The woman in the wheelchair had her head bowed, and
the smoke from the cigarette rose up around her face,
curling under her wire-framed glasses. I watched it gather,
blue and hazy, in the corner of her ceiling. She had raven
black hair streaked with white. Her fist resting on the arm of
her chair was dark as a walnut. She rocked forward very
slowly. "Mr. Younger, I have some questions that no one will
help me with. I want to know the truth about something. I
need a detective."

I sat on the bed, the springs creaked slightly, and I felt the
fur-bearing animal in my stomach twist suddenly toward my
throat.

I don't really think of myself as a disappointment to my
family, but everyone I come into contact with does. They
think of my father as "the sainted Judge Younger." When
they have to talk to me the tone of their voices and their

bloodhound eyes give them away: failure . . . at least the
Judge isn't alive to see it anymore. He was a man who could
give you the whole truth, but as a private investigator the
best I can do is try and create the most acceptable version.
My sister, who is not a failure, is an idealistic law school
professor. She once said to me in the middle of a case, "Don't
confuse the issue with the truth, just develop the facts!" So
much for idealism.

Cops are different, they're right there with sirens screaming and lights flashing, speaking to breathless witnesses
who usually don't have time to think. "Have a seat, ma'am.
You'll feel better if you just tell me the whole truth." It's
weeks, maybe months, by the time I get to them. Impres-
sions have changed to suit opinions, and everyone wants to
become a judge. If cops collect the oral history of a crime, I
gather folklore. And people who have set themselves up to
be the judge rarely accept folklore as the whole truth, unless
it's their own story they're telling.

"Do you need a policeman, Mrs. Victor?"

"I have been to the police. I have been to the district
attorney's. My son has been murdered and I want to know
the whole truth."

I watched the haze of her cigarette smoke clear as a
breath of cold wind blew in through the window. I remembered her son, Louis Victor, the Indian big-game guide. The
Brown Bear Man, shot with a high-powered rifle by a crazy
man. His body had been consumed by the bears near one of
his hunting cabins. The facts were long on irony and short
on conclusions. Sy Brown was the crazy man's attorney. I had
wanted the case, but by that time I had been fired from the
Public Defender Agency and the crazy man couldn't afford
even my violent-crime-of-the-month special of $100 a day.

"Excuse me, Mrs. Victor, but didn't they convict someone of your son's murder? Isn't he already in prison?"

She shook her head slowly. "You don't understand. Maybe you can't. The police told me about the man; he's not right. He talks to himself. He picked up a gun and killed Louis, then left his body for the bears to eat. I know how it happened." She banged her gnarled fist on the arm of the wheelchair. "I want to know why."

"Why—? Mrs. Victor, the man was, is, crazy, unbalanced. He probably doesn't have a reason for killing your son, or at least a reason that you or I can understand. It was a tragic, unforeseeable accident: like an anvil falling out of the sky and killing him."

"White people!" She shook her head bitterly; her nostrils pushed out a squall of smoke. "Anvils do not fall out of the sky."

The bug in my inner ear twitched and I felt the tears coming on. I took in a breath and fought them off.

She leaned forward and pointed her finger at me as if it were a revolver. "My mother could talk to animals. She could talk to the raven and the bear. She talked to the killer whale because the killer whales were our ancestors. But I am a Christian now. I go to the cathedral and if I said I talked to animals you would think I was crazy. I don't talk to animals. I talk to the air and the animals listen."

Behind her the sun dipped behind a cloud and the shadow filtered into the room. Outside her window was a chain-link fence around a flower bed. I saw the raven with the red thread chuckling above a dormant rhododendron.

"Anvils don't fall out of the sky like in some silly cartoon. Someone drops them. I want to pay you, Mr. Younger, to find whoever is responsible for my son's murder."

I looked at my hands and rocked back. I could use the job. If I took it on, I could dig up all the paper on the case, take a couple of days to read it, talk to some of her friends and family and see what she wanted to believe and then give it to her. That's the way it usually works, at least if you want to satisfy your client. It would be a four- or five-hundred-dollar job plus a trip to the prison in Juneau where the largest population of my former clients lives.

"I can look into it for you. I'll need to start gathering the documents in the case file. Do you happen to know the date the man was arrested and what his full name was . . . is?"

She pointed under the bed. There were two cardboard produce cartons full of files and transcripts. "They are all in there, everything, all of the interviews, all of the notes, all of the words from the hearings and the grand jury. I have read them all."

She wheeled herself over to the bed and motioned to the boxes. I lifted one and then the other onto the bed, and she riffled through the files inside the first one.

"There was trouble in my son's family. I'm not sure what it was about but I know he was not happy. He would visit me here and he was a grown man, but he would put his head in his hands just like a little boy and I would tell him stories. He always wanted to hear those Indian stories. I would tell him the same ones my father and uncles told me. The same ones that I tell the grandchildren. He was unhappy just before he died, and I think that he was scared. I think he could see his death. Being crazy is not enough reason for this man to kill Louis. There are other people. This . . . this murder, these papers are not the story. Shouldn't I feel I know the whole truth after I have read two boxes of papers? I don't." She gestured vaguely toward the boxes. "This is not the story of how my son died. This is what the police gave me as an excuse."

She wheeled back to her place by the window. She stared up at me with a startlingly clear expression. There was just the slightest tremor to her head. She fingered the Russian cross on a silver chain around her neck. "How much does it cost to hire you?"

I had never been hired to find out the whole truth before so I had to refigure my time schedule. Since I didn't have to locate the paper on the case I would save time, but if she had actually read it all and still hadn't resolved for herself why it happened, I might have to dig up some outside source to satisfy her. It might be very far outside, and that could take time, and some more of her money.

"That all depends on the type of case and the client. Let me read through the files and see what, if anything, I can do for you. Generally I charge twenty-five dollars per hour plus expenses, and generally no one ever pays their bills so I have to be flexible."

Behind me, there was a knock on the door. I heard it open just a crack. Mrs. Victor looked up.

"One minute! I'll be done in just a minute," she called. "I'm sorry, Mr. Younger, but I have an appointment. Someone is coming to visit. If you could read the files I will pay you two hundred dollars just for your opinion of the case and then we can talk about what to do from there. Can you come and see me tomorrow?"

I nodded, hefted the boxes into my arms, and pried open the door with my knee. There was no one in the hallway waiting to get in so I turned and walked toward the main entrance.

Ordinarily, two fifteen-pound boxes wouldn't be a problem for me but this morning as I teetered down the steps I was breaking into a sweat under my flannel shirt. It was unpleasant. The heat from my body smelled like barroom smoke, and the sweat in my eyes felt like tequila burning under my lids. Even if my body felt like it was rotting, my spirit was beginning to rise. This, at least, was a big case, with some good reading. I wouldn't have to be following somebody in a neck brace, waiting to photograph them playing tennis or jumping on a trampoline. At least this was a murder, even if it was old and already solved.

I walked past the bench. I had too much to carry already so I left the Berry there. It wouldn't be a problem. I had once left *Mind and Nature* on that same bench for a week and no one disturbed it. It was just a little damp and the corners were frayed where it looked like a raven had been turning pages.

TWO

I DON'T LIKE to tell people what I do. They always say, "That must be interesting" and then stare at my chest as if they expect me to pull a gun from under my jacket and dive through the open window out to my waiting car. I don't like to tell people what I do because eventually I disappoint them. I don't drive an expensive car or an old car with lots of character. In fact, I don't have a driver's license. I hitchhike, take cabs, or walk. All three are much better for conversation anyway.

I don't carry a gun. I don't own a handgun, but it seems like there are guns everywhere I work. Look beside the cashbox, behind the bar, the nightstand in the lawyer's bedroom, the cargo pouch of the snowmachine—you'll find one. Large-caliber revolvers mostly, with a solid phallic gravity. But every once in a while there's a small well-made lady's gun.

It's not that I disapprove of handguns; I don't carry one mostly because the police won't let me. They like to picture me knocking on a psychopath's trailer door with nothing but a number 2 pencil, a spiral notebook, and maybe a tape

14

recorder for protection. But it generally works out. The few times I've been able to predict that I'm going to need a gun I take the Judge's long-barreled 12-gauge to the front door. And when the unexpected happens and I am most needy, I wait for the karmic cycle to deliver a piece into my hand. Of course, that hasn't happened, but hope springs eternal.

Physically, I'm also a disappointment as a private investigator. The scar above my right eyebrow is my only dramatic feature. I got it in the sixth grade when Eric Hoffert pushed me into the water fountain. It's the outward sign of my heroic inward suffering.

I like where I live and that hasn't been a disappointment yet: a three-story frame house built on pilings over the water. It has everything I need—office, kitchen, bedroom. Two years ago, we used to flush our toilet and hear the water drop right into the Pacific Ocean under the house. But now the city has a new system so we can flush the toilets and it will travel along an elaborate system of drops and pump stations and be deposited several miles across the island—into the Pacific Ocean. I like where I live, only it seemed a little far away on this particular morning.

I was teetering the boxes down the street, sweating, cursing alcohol, and needing a drink. I stopped in front of the bar and leaned against the wall to talk to a fisherman I knew. I was hoping he would be able to fill me in on what had happened last night—specifically to my charge card. No luck. He had been practicing his saxophone down on his boat all night and he was very excited that he had finally learned to play "In a Sentimental Mood."

He explained that he was a former folk musician taking that twisting musical road into the nineties.

"Pretty twisty," I said, and shouldered my boxes up. I told

him to drop on by and play for me sometime and reminded him not to leave my old Sonny Rollins records next to the exhaust manifold, that my Willie Dixon records had never survived his blues period at sea. I had given all of my records and tapes away and it hadn't occurred to me yet to buy a CD player, but I still didn't like the thought of my treasures being abused.

It was a rare clear morning at the end of October, but it was bound to change. The fishing season was slowing down and most of the boats were in their slips in the harbor. Music was playing from their pilothouses, and the air was filled with the romantic ambiance of gulls calling to the air and diesels blowing out their cooling systems. Someone had had bacon for breakfast, and there were groups of three or four men and women standing around the dock thumbing through engine manuals with their cups of coffee perched on the electrical meters.

Sitka is an island town where people feel crowded by the land and spread out on the sea. This morning to the north and east, the mountains were asserting their presence by showing off the new snow that dusted them down to the two-thousand-foot line. A woman on a troller threw a bucket of breakfast scraps off her back deck and an eagle dove, lifted a blackened crust of bread, and flew off toward the trees where the deserted graveyards lay.

I banged the front door with my feet and Toddy came down the first flight of stairs to help me. Toddy is my roommate—actually, I'm his unofficial guardian. An old friend from Social Services asked me to look out for him until other arrangements could be made. That was two years ago.

He and I were born in the same year under the same sign.

We're 1950 models and Cancers. He has a crew cut, and his glasses have lenses so thick that when he stares up at you, his eyes swim around his face as if he were trying to balance half-dollars in his eye sockets. He is continually sliding his glasses up his nose with his index finger even when he doesn't need to.

I first met Todd in jail. He had been arrested for stealing a pair of shoes and several women's suit coats. When I went to interview him in his cell he was wearing inmate's blue pajamas. His head was shaved and he sat on his bunk, rocking back and forth, twisting his finger as if he were braiding cable.

The police and the shopkeepers never put all of the facts together: Money was never missing, there was never any vandalism, but every so often a gray woman's suit jacket would vanish and once a pair of brown leather pumps was gone from its cardboard box. Store employees were subjected to long straightforward interviews of the "It will be all right if you just want to get it off your chest" variety. It was suggested that a polygraph machine would help them to get it off their chests. But it wasn't until a janitor at the elementary school found a gray woman's suit coat hanging above some sensible shoes in the back of the furnace room that the whole spectacular crime unraveled. Todd, an assistant janitor at the time, was sitting behind the hot-water heater with his head in his hands, weeping.

After he was placed under arrest, the police prided themselves upon solving a particularly puzzling crime. The Social Services people were assured that their suspicions about Todd were well founded. He was designated as a "person in need of aid," handcuffed, and taken to the jail.

Some people say Todd is retarded. At Social Services

they said he was "mentally and emotionally challenged," but the woman who used to love me said he had too gentle a heart to live in the real world.

He was charged with criminal mischief. I was sent by his attorney to talk to him about his defense. First I had to go to the law library and find out what the elements of criminal mischief were and then interview Todd and see if it was true that he was a mischievous criminal. I intended to talk to him about times, places, motives, and maybe an alibi; instead he told me about his mother.

Todd's mother had been a teacher at the elementary school; his father had been a mechanic working out in the logging camps. When he was six, they had ridden on a friend's small troller out to the logging camp at False Island. After his dad finished work on one of the light plant generators, he and some of his friends in camp went down to the dock to drink and listen to the radio. They were drinking beer and whiskey, telling stories, and every once in a while when a good song came on through the static, his dad would grab his mother and spin her around on the dock to dance. Todd remembered how her laughter seemed to bubble out of her mouth like birdsong. He was laughing when his father twirled her an extra flip and she fell into the bay, and everyone was laughing when they hauled her out. She stood with water beading off the strands of her hair, embarrassed and shivering, trying to giggle. Someone gave her another drink of whiskey to warm her up. It was a cool fall afternoon and everyone thought she was going down below to change her clothes, but when someone checked on her later they laughed again because she had passed out with her wet clothes on. The radio played up on the dock and Todd sat down below in the boat watching her teeth chatter. He was worried when he saw that she'd broken one of her teeth chattering so hard. He put a blanket over her. He wished his father would come, but gradually he stopped worrying when she stopped shivering. I'm not sure if he realized he had watched his mother die of hypothermia, but, if he did, it didn't seem to bother him because his mother had since told him not to worry.

The cell was the green cement of an old railroad station. The bunks were metal slats and damp blankets. The tags that said, "Do not remove under penalty of law" were missing from the mattresses. On the back wall was an elaborate chalk drawing of a trolling boat with its poles down, lines in the water, sailing toward a black setting sun. Underneath in blue ink someone had written "Seiners Suck." There was a radio playing, and the guy in the next cell was doing pushups to the beat of a Bruce Springsteen song.

"It's a funny thing," Todd said, and he squinted at me. "When Jesus was alive, how was he connected to the earth? By his feet, just like the rest of us, except he didn't wear shoes because his spirit went right into the ground like lightning. But most of the rest of us wear shoes so it keeps us from grounding out. Ever notice how it hurts most people to walk barefooted but the people in the Bible go barefoot so easy—that's because they're ready to be hit by lightning."

The radio in the next cell had switched to a country western ballad, and the inmate was doing situps.

Todd spoke a little more softly. "If I arrange the shoes just right somewhere my mom might have stood, God will hover there like a little mist. He doesn't speak, he doesn't even look like anything except maybe a little rain cloud, but"— he sat forward and his body relaxed as if the words were an exhalation of a long-held breath—"if I hang a coat above the shoes, the mist fills up her clothes and Momma can talk to me from heaven. But only if I arrange the shoes in just the right place in a particular way. It would be crazy to do it otherwise."

He told me about the place in the furnace room where his mother had told him what heaven was like and about all the gifts she was saving to give him when she saw him again. She made him promise never to tell anyone else what heaven was like because it would make life on earth that much harder. In fact, she had regretted telling Todd the details of heaven and that was why he was crying when the janitor walked in on them. His momma had told him she was not going to talk to him anymore. She was worried that he wanted to be in heaven more than he wanted to be on the earth. She said that God wanted him to be on earth a little longer. "You are all I have left on earth," she told him and then began to fade into the furnace pipes and asbestos insulation.

I read somewhere that when a child realizes his favorite doll cannot speak back to him, there is a silence that fills the mind. There was Toddy, with nothing of his greatest love but some stolen shoes and a suit jacket, and the world was very quiet.

I sat in the cell with him. The inmate next door had turned off his radio and was stretching. I felt a little uncomfortable, and I didn't quite know what to ask next. But there was one thing I wanted to know.

"What is heaven like?"

He held his hands palms up and looked sad and apologetic. "It's funny," he said, "but since she left I can't remember a thing about heaven. Not pictures or anything, only feelings sometimes. Feelings . . . like I can almost remember but I'm not sure. Do you know what I mean?"

"I think I do."

The door banged against the wall. "Todd, get one of these boxes, would you, pal?"

"Sure, Cecil. I was just listening to the radio and looking at books about how they pumped air into the hull of the *Titanic* and about how you can avoid getting the bends. Do you know those bubbles when you open a pop bottle? Well, that's like what happens when you get the bends."

Todd was wearing bib overalls and a forest green jersey underneath. He had his down booties on, so it was a good bet he had spent the morning under an afghan reading the encyclopedia.

I kicked off my leather slip-on shoes and put on my house slippers. We both started padding up the stairs. I wanted to smell some coffee.

"Those bubbles get in your blood and they can cause extreme discomfort."

"I can imagine. Listen, we got any coffee?"

I looked out the windows above the sink overlooking the channel. A beautiful steel-hulled crab boat was passing, gulls diving in its wake. I noticed there was coffee on, and Toddy had done all the breakfast dishes. I walked over and took a mug down from one of the brass hangers.

"Cecil, do you think you could salvage boats from underwater? It is very dangerous and there is a great amount of discomfort involved, but very often it can be quite lucrative."

"I don't know, Todd. I bet between the two of us we could get it done. But, listen, do you think you could turn down the radio some? I've got to read all the crap in these boxes, and I'll have to make some phone calls."

"You have another case, Cecil?"

"You don't have to ask in such a tone of shock, do you? I have plenty of cases. They're mostly inactive at this point."

"Sunken," Toddy murmured, and he chuckled as he padded toward the radio.

"Funny! To answer your question, I don't know if I have a new case or not. It might be more storytelling than investigation."

"Will it be quite lucrative?"

"Excessively lucrative, Todd, and particularly free of extreme discomfort. So much better than raising sunken ships."

I sat on the couch facing the woodstove. It had started to rain, which is what it mostly does in southeastern Alaska in October. The stove created a pleasant bubble of heat in the room. The rain sounded like birds dancing on the tin roof. I was drinking coffee with half-and-half and as the afternoon progressed I added one small shot of Irish Cream. Todd flipped through the T's and listened to the radio while I read the history on Louis Victor's murder.

In May of 1982, Louis Victor had hired a young farmhand from Illinois named Alvin Hawkes. Hawkes worked as a deckhand on the charter boat. Victor needed an errand boy to help meet the needs of the German industrialists who come to Alaska and pay an average of ten thousand dollars for the privilege of shooting a brown bear with a high-powered rifle. Hawkes also packed lunches, filled gas tanks, and started lunch fires on the beach to warm the clients.

There were several people who came forward later to say that Hawkes seemed strange; that he talked to himself, and would sometimes stand alone and seem to be arguing with himself. There was a transcription of telephonic testimony from a well-known Hollywood actor who had been a client of Victor's. He told the grand jury that at the time he thought Hawkes "had a screw loose" but he had never mentioned it to anyone until contacted by the district attorney's office.

On October 2, 1982, Hawkes was supplying a remote hunting cabin on Admiralty Island. Hawkes had stayed in the cabin for a week, cutting wood and hiking, trying to get a fix on the bears in the area. For ten thousand dollars you don't want just any bear, you need to take home the skin of an awesome man-eater, the only other slavering omnivore in North America. And you don't want to walk too far to find it. So the guides learn the habits of the local bears to give their clients the shortest walk and the best shot.

On October 3, Louis Victor received a radio transmission from Hawkes that sounded like he was in some kind of trouble. Victor and his two adult children, Lance and Norma, took their boat, the *Oso*, from Juneau up into Seymour Canal on Admiralty Island. A close family friend, Walter Robbins, traveled with them in his own vessel along with his daughter De De, who was his deckhand that season before she started college. It was early evening when they arrived.

Robbins said in his statement that he saw Louis go ashore with his rifle to speak with Hawkes. The next morning,

Alvin Hawkes was raving about how Louis Victor had gone crazy and tried to kill him and then had run off into the woods. Hawkes had a cut across his cheek and a bruise where it appeared he had been hit with a blunt instrument. There was blood on his shirt and a great deal of blood on the steps and door latch of the cabin. Hawkes maintained that all of the blood was his own, and that Louis had attacked him with a splitting maul.

There was a statement from Lance Victor that he had seen Hawkes throw a rifle into the bay early that morning. Lance showed the state troopers where the rifle had been thrown. Later, a dive team recovered it from the water.

I flipped through a dozen packets of 3-by-5 color prints: Shots of the cabin from the air. Shots of the cabin from the water. Shots of blood spattered on the outside of the door. Shots of troopers holding rulers next to blood spattered on the doorjamb. Shots of gray hair caught in the splinters on the edge of the chopping block. And shots of the rifle. It was a 45–70, not the most common caliber in this part of the country, but it was the rifle that Louis Victor carried when he hunted Sitka blacktail deer.

They found Louis Victor's body lying in the grassy flats of an estuary about half a mile from the cabin. His body had been partially consumed by brown bears.

There were some notes back and forth from the FBI and some bear experts at the university in Fairbanks. The experts expressed the opinion that it was unusual for a brown bear to have destroyed the body, and the only possible way to explain it would be if the man was dead before being consumed. Brown bears won't eat their human prey, it seems; black bears do.

The photographs of the body were 8-by-10, in color,

showing long strands of meat clinging to the skeletal remains of an upper torso. The thin bones of the sternum had
been snapped into splinters where the bears had rooted
around in the chest cavity snuffling up Louis's internal
organs. The cuffs of his blue wool shirt were still intact
around his wrists. His head was shorn of its scalp where a
massive paw had slapped across it. The bone of the skull
was glaring white. The head was propped on a rock, and the
eyes in the sockets were brown, the lids gone, the eyes
staring at the photographer as if in shock.

I imagined the D.A. putting those pictures in the files to
give to the victim's mother: "The meddling old bitch wants to
see everything, we'll show her everything."

There were transcripts of four interviews the state
troopers had conducted with Hawkes on the fourth, fifth,
seventh, and tenth. On the fourth, Hawkes seemed nervous.
He was stammering, and he must have moved around the
interview room a lot, because he showed up as "unintelligible response" on the typed transcripts, but he stuck to his
story: Louis had gone crazy and had come at him with a
splitting maul. They had struggled briefly, and when
Hawkes had slugged him, Louis had run into the woods.
Hawkes knew nothing about a killing.

The transcripts of the fifth and seventh showed a much
more nervous Hawkes. His stuttering was more pro-
nounced, and he blurted out non sequiturs as if speaking to
someone not in the room: "Shut up, you bastards." It was
noted that Hawkes shook his head violently and kept digging in his ear with a wooden match, repeating: "Shut up,
you bastards."

On the ninth, the autopsy report was released, indicating
that Louis Victor had been killed by a gunshot wound in the

head. There were no powder burns nor signs of heavy bruising, indicating the shot was not fired at close range. The entry wound was a small hole below the right eye that originally had been mistaken for the puncture of a large canine tooth.

On the tenth, Hawkes spit out his words in spraying stutters. The typist who had worked on the tape was clearly struggling; she punctuated his comments with question marks in parentheses. Hawkes claimed to be an agent of "a great power." He heard voices generated from the center of the earth. A transmitter had been implanted in his inner ear at birth, and this allowed Alvin Hawkes to hear the instructions. He had tried to explain to Louis Victor that the voices had foretold his death. The voices had said that Louis would be killed by the great power. He would be killed, he had to be killed. And wasn't Victor now dead? Didn't that prove that he was telling the truth—that the voices always told the truth? They foretold the future perfectly, perfectly.

In Alaska, there is no insanity defense that's worth anything to a defendant, so the troopers weren't worried about that, but they were worried about the fact that Hawkes seemed to be confessing before he had answered yes to the Miranda questions as to whether he understood his rights. The typed transcript of the last interview was obviously more worn than the others, and the critical statements constituting his Miranda warnings were marked in yellow, probably the work of Hawkes's attorney.

The interview had started off as a friendly talk. "You understand, Alvin, we just need to clear things up. You were there. You can help us. Now, Alvin, you have the right to remain silent. Anything you say can and will be used against you in a court of law. You have the right to an attorney. . . . Do you understand, Alvin? Do you understand?"

Although Hawkes had answered yes to several questions, including the one about the Miranda warnings, whether he understood them was left open, since by the end of the interview the transcripts indicated "unintelligible sobbing" and profanity: "Oh, Jesus fucking Christ. Christ. Oh, Jesus."

For the next six months, Alvin Hawkes underwent a battery of psychological evaluations while he was in custody. His court-appointed lawyer decided to make the question of his sanity moot and tried to force a deal with the D.A. to reduce the charge to manslaughter by threatening to take the case to trial on the self-defense issue. Crazy or not, Hawkes's story seemed to be that he had been attacked by Louis after he had given Louis the disturbing news from the center of the earth. He had been attacked by Louis and had fought back in self-defense.

There had been a witness to the fight. Walt Robbins's daughter, eighteen-year-old De De, had been on deck while her father's boat was anchored in the bay. De De Robbins told police investigators and the grand jury that she had seen two men fighting in front of the cabin after Louis went ashore. She had seen them wrestle out the door and then roll back into the cabin. She thought it looked more like horseplay than a real fight. She went down to the forward berth where her father was sleeping. He had gone below shortly after dinner. Walt and De De pulled anchor early the next morning to go hunting. They only came back to the cabin when they heard the emergency radio transmissions from the *Oso* to the state troopers' office in Juneau.

The D.A. wanted murder one and tampering with evidence: Hawkes had dragged the body to the estuary to destroy the evidence of the crime. The defense attorney was holding out for a manslaughter plea bargain. Otherwise, he would take it all the way and either try to get Hawkes off on a Miranda-violation motion or make the state try him on the self-defense angle. He intended to keep Hawkes off the stand and introduce the first taped statement because Hawkes wouldn't sound as crazy as he would if the D.A. got hold of him on cross-examination. The jury would love the crying on the tape.

The best part of a murder trial is the victim never gets a chance to testify.

I poured a little more Irish Cream into my cold coffee. Todd got up and turned off the radio and went to the refrigerator to pour himself some milk. Up to this point, the case seemed unremarkable, although it did seem to have some sad touches of drama. But as I read the next section of the file I had a funny reaction: In spite of my hangover and the first blurring effects of the Irish Cream, my skin crawled like I had just eaten some bad Chinese food.

On the eve of the trial, De De Robbins, the only defense witness, was found floating next to a pier off the docks in Bellingham, Washington. Friends had seen her walking out of a rock concert with a date. The witnesses stated that they thought De De and her date had been drinking, they appeared to be weaving and stumbling. The autopsy indicated an elevated blood-alcohol level. There were pictures of her body on the stainless steel examining table. She was milky white, and the insides of her arms and her chest were abraded with scratches and bruises where, it appeared, she had tried to pull herself out of the water by climbing up one of the mussel-encrusted pilings. In one shot her head was tossed back and hidden from the camera by the strands of wet hair clinging to her face. The next shot showed her full face: lifeless eyes open, stunned and afraid.

There was a memo from the Bellingham Police Department speculating as to whether Alvin Hawkes could somehow be tied in to an organized-crime network. The state troopers couldn't work up much enthusiasm for that theory, so they focused on the defense attorney, Sy Brown. Could he have wanted to win the case so badly that he would arrange a key witness's death?

"She was *my* witness. Why in the hell would I want her dead? Grow up." That brief message was handwritten on a yellow memo pad.

Two days after her death, De De's father, who'd claimed the body, was packing up her room. He read the diary that was inside her night-table drawer. In the entries for the last five days of her life she had written that she was worried about a doctor's appointment. She didn't know how Rudy would deal with the situation, if it went the wrong way. She'd written poems, rhymed couplets, asking God to take care of her and Rudy and "please not to give us gifts that we are not ready for." The last entry was written in an uneven scrawled hand. It said that she had prayed a lot and had decided she couldn't live without her baby. There was a photocopy of this page. The last two lines read, "There are so many lies— there are so many lies. There is nothing I can do. Papa, do you understand? There is nothing I can do."

The autopsy report, stapled to the police report, indicated that the corpse had been a pregnant female Caucasian.

There was also a police summary indicating that the police had talked to De De's boyfriend (in his wife's presence), and he had reported that on the evening of her death, De De had been extremely upset, had been drinking, and had gone out to meet someone else. He didn't know whom and apparently he didn't care.

In a letter to the Alaska death investigators, the Bellingham Police Department reported that, as a result of their investigation, they had concluded that De De Robbins had committed suicide. The findings were based not only on the diary and the police reports, but on statements from her college classmates, all saying she was "despondent during the last few days of her life," and from her boyfriend, Rudolfo Anastanso, a Filipino floor-covering contractor, who was in the process of separation from his wife at the time of De De's death.

With the death of the only independent witness (and maybe because of a little fear of the official heat created by the Robbins death investigation), the defense attorney folded. On July 7, he pleaded Hawkes guilty but mentally ill to the murder two count and to the offense of tampering with evidence.

But there was one last surprise. The D.A. produced several doctors who had examined Hawkes. They testified that while Hawkes "had suffered periodic psychotic episodes, he was not currently legally insane. The best therapy for him would be to serve whatever sentence seemed appropriate not in the Alaska mental-health system but in the correctional system." Hawkes was crazy, but not crazy enough.

Sy Brown had been taken by surprise by the state's assertion that Hawkes was sane. I read through a flurry of official memos from him to the Department of Law.

One from Brown read, "If this guy is so sane, how about a third-party work release into your custody?"

The response: "He's not crazy and you know it. He's just your basic murderer. We might consider a twenty-four-hour release to you. It's going to be a long winter for the bears."

There were others complaining about the ethics of surprise tactics and about the propriety of handshake agreements when dealing with the "protection of the citizens of the state."

The memos never changed a thing. Hawkes went down hard. On October 15, 1982, he was sentenced to forty years for murder two and five years for tampering with evidence. His case wasn't appealed on the Miranda issue.

Hawkes is presently being held at Lemon Creek jail until he can be shipped to Leavenworth where he will serve no less than three-fourths of his original sentence: thirty years of Salisbury steak and instant mashed potatoes, weight lifting, skull picks made from toothbrushes, and listening to the voices scream inside his head.

THREE

IT WAS FIVE o'clock, pitch dark and raining outside. I stood and looked out the window to the channel. There was a little wooden troller at the fuel dock and a skiff was running toward the fish plant dock. Through the dock lights I could see the driver of the skiff was wearing bulky yellow rain gear and had a tarp across his lap. The lights of the Pioneer Home reflected in the water of his wake.

After I was fired from the Public Defender Agency in Juneau I was out of commission for a while and then came to Sitka. It seemed foolish to the people in Juneau, some of whom I had grown up with. They said I could never run a business in Sitka. It's only about seventy miles by air from Juneau but to Juneauites Sitka is almost the Third World. For all of its historic charm and Tlingit/Russian heritage, it's a hick town. "Come on," they said, "mysterious blondes never go to Sitka when they want to hire a detective to find the rare coin stolen from their father's mansion." It's true. But still, I seem to get enough of the work that keeps me busy. Rape, assault, an occasional murder, always for the defense, and an occasional personal injury civil suit. I don't do divorces or insurance work unless I'm completely broke, which is about four times a year. I don't do all that much of my work in Sitka but travel out of town. Because of my reputation, I can't charge what most of the ex-cop-type investigators get, so I get work from skinflints from all over the state who don't care as much about reputation as they do about billings. I'm not too disappointed that I don't do much work in Sitka because I'm not liked all that well around here as it is, without having every sex offender who surfaces in my new hometown as a client.

Having a lot of enemies has few advantages, but one of them is being able to trust the couple of friends that you have. My friends have to suffer some public humiliation just by being associated with me, and that gives us a certain esprit de corps not enjoyed by people with more morally comfortable lives. We judge each other by what we don't have as a consequence of being together, what we've given up. It was pointed out—rather dramatically—by the woman who used to love me that this was a bonding based on emotional and spiritual poverty. She laid these insights on me about six months ago as she was leaving. She said she wanted more than ego, irony, and alcohol. I agreed, but I couldn't imagine what was left—other than silliness, and maybe despair. She walked out the door. I waited ten minutes and then went to the bar.

The bar was where I was headed now. My eyes were tired. I had read enough and needed to hear a good story about Louis Victor's murder. The particular bar that I was walking to was the Beinecke Rare Book Library of gossip. The walls are lined with photographs of fishing boats, and the ceiling is studded with dollar bills tacked to the chipped acoustical tiles. If I was lucky, and if today was like any other of the three hundred and sixty-four, I would find the master of the *Julie M.* in his booth by the package-goods store. His name is William; he's my friend, and also the curator of the gossip collection.

As I walked in, he was talking with a young woman fisherman. William has long gray sideburn whiskers that he ties under his chin. He was wearing an insulated canvas work suit. She wore a thermal underwear shirt, black jeans, rubber boots, and a purple beret. She was drunkenly describing a mule ride in the jungles of Costa Rica. She reeled back in the booth and fixed her eyes on the tropical distance, describing the slap in the face of a palm frond. William smiled into his plum brandy and pushed the frond from his face with his forearms. I held up two fingers to the barmaid and made a circular gesture in the direction of William's booth. The barmaid nodded, and I went over to sit down.

"Cecil Younger, the subarctic gumshoe, have you ever considered opening a fishing lodge in Costa Rica?"

"Can't say as I have, William. Mind if I sit down?"

The woman with the beret looked up in surprise at finding me so suddenly in the jungle and said, "Well, if you don't want to open a fishing lodge then just fuck off, both of you." She stood up and began a port tack to the other end of the bar.

"An excitable child," William said. "But she knows Costa Rica. Business or pleasure, Cecil? If you're here to ask me what I know about the shoplifting, I'm a dead end for you."

"Shoplifting?"

"Today at the gun shop. Someone ran out of the store with a hunting rifle. The police have been tearing up the waterfront."

"No, I don't know anything about that. I'm here to buy you a drink and see if you know any good stories."

"Plentee stories, the finest kine!" William said in mock Hawaiian pidgin.

"What do you know about Louis Victor and Walt Robbins?"

William smiled up at me and twisted the braid that was tied under his chin while he acknowledged the drinks the barmaid brought to the table.

"A murder, is it? Well, you know the basics, I take it." He didn't wait for me to answer.

"Louis and Walt grew up in Juneau together. They stuck out; Walt took a lot of teasing for being friends with this Indian kid. Walt was a year or two younger, I think. Louis was a better hunter, or at least he brought more and bigger game in. Louis was better with the women and always seemed to have more money. I always kind of suspected that it was humiliating for Walt to work for Louis all those years. Louis made his money on the North Slope, enough to buy his guide business.

"I've heard rumors that Walt was sleeping with Emma, Louis's wife. I don't buy that. Emma's a knotty piece of wet rope. I don't think she could loosen up even if she wanted to."

"Did Robbins want in on the hunting territory?"

"Yeah, I guess Walt wanted that territory. It was great bear hunting, it had a fair anchorage."

"Enough to kill Louis?"

William drank the last of his brandy. "How the fuck should I know?" He looked down into his drink. "I don't think he killed Louis. Louis was an Indian and he was kind of arrogant but Walt loved him." He pulled the tip of his finger around the rim of the glass. "And, anyway, the facts don't fit all that well. Walt had passed out on his boat. And even if he wanted to kill Louis for the permit, Emma inherited it after Louis's death and Emma hates Walt's guts. The poor bastard. I heard he offered to buy the outfit and permit for three times what it's worth but Emma wouldn't let him in the door. I mean, I don't know. I just heard that Emma and Louis had their own troubles. But Walt never got his foot in the door, that I know."

"Someone said that Robbins was already in Bellingham when his daughter committed suicide."

"I never heard that. I heard that Walt was up here. You're not fishing on me, are you, Younger? Man, you are sick—but I like it. Robbins was worried about her, I know that. She was sleeping with some Filipino guy. It bugged the shit out of him. But he would never have killed her. Robbins is supposed to be kind of flipped out ever since she died."

He waved down the barmaid, and signaled for two more brandies. "But, Cecil, you just can't get around the wacko. You know, Louis was big—there's a story that he and Walt were once jumped by a brown bear sow and Louis wrestled it before Walt killed it. You'd have to be a pretty husky motherfucker to wrestle a sow. But I hear this wacko was huge—six six or something. They say he tried to eat Louis himself."

I hate plum brandy but I drink it out of consideration for William. I swallowed the last of it and set the glass on the other side of the table. "You believe that about the wacko?"

"Cecil, my boy, I know you haven't come to me for the truth. I just tell you the story."

Someone put money in the jukebox next to our table and we had to stop our conversation. We sat with our backs to the wall. William knotted his whiskers and watched the lady in the beret. Like a dope, I began to trace the rim of my empty glass with an index finger and listen to the wheezy dance tune blare out.

I should never have given all of my music away after she left me.

We drank until about eight. The Costa Rican fishing-lodge entrepreneur returned and forgave us briefly for our lack of judgment, and then she started talking about black-cod fishing in the Gulf of Alaska and hiking the Napali coast of Kauai, which were two related subjects in her mind.

I took a walk around the bar and heard a story of how they diagnose transmission trouble in California by swinging a crystal over the drive train. I heard a story about the crew having sex with a goat on the deck of a whaling ship in the South Pacific. I heard about a skipper who spent his fifty thousand dollars of halibut money on cocaine, and didn't regret it a bit. This is a great bar. You can't believe a thing anyone says, but you have to take them seriously. When I left, William was riding the back of the booth as if it were a mule and the woman in the beret was leading him down the steep terrain of Kauai.

Right now the whole story of Louis Victor belonged in the same dream world as the jungles of Costa Rica. What William had told me was a story like all the others—who knew where it came from? But I might be able to find it useful in selling an acceptable version to my client.

Todd had supper ready when I walked through the door. I could smell halibut under the broiler. I padded up the stairs, holding the rail as if it were a mule's saddle horn. I could hear Todd reading aloud from the encyclopedia about the sunken ships of the North Atlantic while he stirred the rice.

He held the book very close to his face, his eyeballs swimming across the page.

"Some ships went down with all hands lost. Cecil, do you think there could have been any wild animals on board those ships? I mean, could a zoo or something have been shipping some animal from Africa or somewhere? I'd hate to think of that. I would hate to think of that—monkeys or zebras going down in a ship, in their cages and all. Do you think it ever happened?"

"I don't think it ever did, Todd, and, anyway, I think they make cages so they'll float free of the ship if it sinks, and they have radios attached to them so they will be easy to find. I wouldn't worry." Once Todd worried so much about the wild animals in a traveling carnival he was almost arrested for pulling grass from people's lawns to take over to the cages to feed to them. "I wouldn't worry, Todd. I think the new cages float."

Just as we were about to sit down and eat, the phone rang. A woman who spoke in a very strained tone of voice was on the line.

"Mr. Younger, my name is Emma Victor, and I believe you've been hired by my mother-in-law to investigate the facts surrounding the death of my husband."

The rice was boiling over and Todd was frantically looking for a pot holder. I reached in the drawer beside the sink and gave him one.

"That's correct. May I ask how you knew that?"

"I live with my family here in Juneau but I speak to my mother-in-law quite frequently. In fact, I spoke to her by phone just this afternoon and she told me about your . . . commission, I suppose you'd call it."

The rice was calmed down, but now it needed more water

and Todd was having trouble holding the pot over the sink and turning on the water. I reached over and twisted the spigot.

"Yes—is there something I can do for you?"

"It is very important that I talk to you, Mr. Younger. In fact, I might have some information that could . . . drastically affect your work. I can't go into it over the phone. Could we meet here in Juneau sometime? Will you be coming here soon? As I said, it is very important that I talk to you."

"I hadn't planned on making any trips right away but I'm sure I could arrange something."

"Good. I live at the twenty-four-mile post on Tee Harbor. I know that you know Juneau. Our number is in the book. Call and come out. I'll phone you day after tomorrow if I haven't heard from you before then. All right?"

And she hung up. Her voice lingered like the whine of a dentist's drill.

"Who was it?" Todd asked.

"I guess it was the daughter-in-law of my new client. She called me from Juneau and acted like she wanted to talk but she didn't want to get into much of a conversation over the phone."

Todd set the rice and the halibut on the table and just as we sat down someone knocked on the door.

Todd pushed up from the table. "I'll get it, Cecil," he said, and I watched him lumber downstairs.

His voice came up from the stairwell. "Cecil, there is someone here to see you."

"Who is it? Send them up."

"They say they need to talk to you outside."

I could hear Todd walking back up the stairs. He walks

methodically like an experienced mountain climber pacing himself on the lower slopes. First I saw his bristly head and then his eyeballs behind his glasses.

"I don't know who he is, Cecil. He won't come in. He won't even come close to the door. He just sort of stands back in the dark—kind of grumbling."

We walked down the stairs together. The room on the street level is a mudroom, with rain gear hanging from pegs and red rubber boots lining the wall. There is a large window in the yellow cedar door to the street and a white curtain hanging across the window for privacy. With the street light on, you should be able to see the silhouette of a person standing at the front door. There was no one. We looked at each other. Toddy frowned.

"I'm sorry, Cecil, but there was somebody. There really was." He walked to the door. "He was standing right here, kind of in the street, just a second ago. I couldn't see very well but it was a skinny person standing back in the dark. I didn't make it up."

Todd opened the door and stepped out.

"His voice was all gravelly and I couldn't see him very . . ."

His head rocked back against the doorjamb. At first I thought he'd stumbled. I put my arms under his armpits to steady him and we both slumped to the floor.

"Toddy?"

I was surprised that he seemed so limp, and then the back of his shirt felt damp. I looked at his face. His glasses were on. His eyes were closed. There was a small hole in the middle of his jersey above his overalls, and there was a hole the size of a softball under his shoulder blade. I raised my hand up to my face and it was sparkly and red as if in a vivid dream.

I remember a squeal building up from my lungs. I remember blood drying in his hair and under my fingernails. I remember the smell of the ocean, the sound of the gulls . . . and then sirens.

FOUR

WHEN THEY FIRST arrived they shook me down, looking
for the weapon. They spread me on the sidewalk and frisked
me, asking questions about cocaine and my drug connec-
tions. I lay still with my cheek pressing down onto the
cement, watching the thick soles on black shoes. Men and
women arrived with the ambulance. There were tackle
boxes and many packages of gauze. Men giving orders in
urgent whispers. Blue and red lights pulsing, tubes, IV
bottles and a stretcher. They loaded Todd into the ambulance. They took me to the police station.

They told me to get a hold of myself. That I would feel
better if I told them everything; that nothing could change
what had happened but I could change what would happen
from here on out if I would just level with them.

If I had been in a little better shape, I would have
answered with swelteringly pithy epithets. But I just told
them to look around on the hill behind my house for a high-
powered shell casing. Beyond that they could fuck off.

They gave me a cup of coffee in a Styrofoam cup and a
pair of jail pants because they needed my blue jeans, which

were sticky with Todd's blood. They also gave me lots of slow, steady stares as if I were a piece of rotting meat sitting in their station.

They knew I didn't shoot him but they also knew they wouldn't mind if they could prove that I had. In most small towns, if a crime is committed and it isn't painfully obvious who did it, the rule of thumb is to grab the nearest slimeball, so at least you'll have something to show the D.A.'s office on Monday morning. I was the nearest slimeball.

It was about 10:00 P.M. when Detective Lester Bloom walked into the combination kitchenette and interview room behind the first lockup and said that my loudmouth Jewish lawyer was outside.

My attorney, Dickie Stein, is a rabid terrier, who has a flexible attitude toward reality. The police hate him unless they need to hire him to represent them after they've been sued for aggressively counseling prisoners in their cells. He walked in: red high-top sneakers, blue jeans, and an Albert Einstein T-shirt that said, "186,000 MILES PER SECOND ISN'T JUST A GOOD IDEA, IT'S THE LAW." He sat down.

"What the fuck?"

"Somebody shot Toddy, rifle shot, some distance, never heard a thing. Man—woman, I don't know. I guess they wanted me."

"How come?"

I shrugged. I didn't want to think about it.

"The cops are questioning all of the store owners where Todd stole those clothes."

"Figures. Is anyone taking time out from making brilliant motivational analyses to check the scene? Did they find the rifle that was stolen from the gun shop yet? Any shell casings, footprints? Or are they hoping to save time by beating a confession out of some of the girls down at the clothing store?"

"They'll get to it. You know how they like to work. So, you need a lawyer?"

"Ask the police."

"They're bored already with the thought of sending you to prison. All they've got is a vague description of a guy stealing a rifle earlier today and you, in jail. This is going to be a semi-big deal around here, you know. Somebody's going to have to go down. Maybe, even if you didn't shoot him, they might just want to hold on to you. Maybe to see what's in the toilet after you piss if nothing else. Right now they want to hold you on a firearms violation. So, you want to talk to an attorney?"

"Firearms violation! I want a drink, Dickie. I need to do some more reading and talk to a few people before I can tell you anything. Listen, just get me out of here and as soon as I know something I'll tell you."

"Have they taken any pictures of your face?"

"Yeah, when I first came in. I had blood all over it."

"Any bruises?"

"No."

"Too bad, but I'll see what I can do."

I waited in the kitchenette, I drank coffee and tried to scrape the blood out from under my fingernails with the tines of a plastic fork. After about twenty minutes Bloom came in, his stomach peeking out from where his shirt should have been tucked.

"It doesn't look like we'll be needing anything more from you tonight, Mr. Younger. We're going over the physical evidence and we'll be in touch."

"You're supposed to say 'Don't leave town.'"

"Don't leave town."

"I'm going to Juneau tomorrow. You can reach me at Lemon Creek."

Bloom worked on a sly grin.

"You figure you might as well go check yourself into jail now? Awful nice of you to help us out, Cecil."

"Let's get out of here, Dickie, before he asks me to squeal like a pig."

As we walked out of the police station, Dickie stopped and talked with the chief, who was shaking off his raincoat as he came in the door. Dickie assured him he could work something out with me so I wouldn't pursue a claim against the city for being slapped around by Bloom when I was brought in.

"Not real bright to take pictures of the bloody prisoner, Ed. I can take care of it, but you'll owe me one. Okay?"

The chief thanked him and promised to have a talk with Bloom. Bloom was just getting the gag, and he didn't look particularly happy. His face was taking on the character of a basset hound standing in the rain. I didn't wave as we walked out.

I left Dickie at the intersection and walked up the hill to the hospital. The nurse at the night station told me Todd was in room 203 but that he couldn't have any visitors. Then she looked at me and at my bloody shirt and my prison pants. Then she said he had just gotten out of the E.R. and someone from the state troopers was in with him now. They were going to do emergency surgery as soon as the surgical team arrived. I told her I was with Todd's attorney and that the troopers had asked me to come down. I told her this over my shoulder. She began to yell at me as my hand turned the knob of room 203.

George Doggy sat next to Toddy's bed, changing the batteries in his backup tape machine while he rewound the tape on the machine plugged into a socket. He was wearing a strange outfit of running pants, a T-shirt, and a tweed jacket. His gray hair was wet and uncombed. It looked like he had come from his workout.

Doggy had been around since before statehood. He had been involved in every successful investigation the state ever ran. When the time came, he didn't want to retire, so the state sent him to Sitka to be a consultant to the police academy, which is the statewide training center for all the law enforcement in Alaska. As far as I could tell, he mostly walked around in his sweats carrying his athletic bag. But they kept him on the payroll and when something interesting came along anywhere in the state, the commissioner in Juneau sent Doggy out to "ease around the investigation" and report back to him.

When I first started doing defense investigations I had the idea that all cops in Alaska were ape-like creatures without enough integrity to keep their jobs as bouncers in the pipeline strip joints where most of them came from. And for the first few years of doing traffic accidents and nickel-bag drug cases this image held up pretty well. Doggy changed that. He only had to report to one man plus the governor. And all of the governors since statehood were scared of him. They were never sure how much he knew and they were never sure they wanted to know. He hated politics and political pressure but he understood them both, and there was speculation that he thoroughly documented any loose

political talk that came his way, and a lot must have passed
by him over the years. Doggy rarely kept notes but he was
always covered. He wasn't afraid to admit a mistake and
he didn't care if a defense lawyer tromped on his ego
but he never got caught in a contradiction or a knowing lie.
This put him up there with Buddha as far as most police
investigators were concerned. Doggy didn't play games
and he knew that "just the facts" could be a twisty mess that
would take a cop with patience and intelligence a long time
to unravel.

"He can't talk now, Cecil." Doggy unplugged the machine and began curling the cord around his fist. He looked
the way men in good shape look when they are called out on
a job late at night, tired but healthy.

"They're not going to ship him to Seattle. It's bad, but not
worth the risk of transporting him. He looks like a strong
kid."

My clothes were stained with Todd's blood. My shirt was
stiff with it and I smelled like a soggy meat wrapper. My
head hurt and I was having trouble focusing.

Doggy smiled up at me, and motioned for me to sit. "I
think they are going to want your clothes."

I nodded.

"Did they interview you already?"

"Yeah. They acted a little disappointed that I didn't break
down and confess so they could get back to their TV shows."

"Now, Cecil, you know they don't have a lot to work with."
And he smiled again. "What do you think?"

I buried my head in my hands and then stared down at
his running shoes. "I don't know, Doggy. He said it was
somebody with a scratchy voice at the door who wanted to
talk to me. He didn't know who it was."

"They found a shell casing near the Russian blockhouse across the way from your place. It's a .308. It's a good thing it didn't hit him solidly but more or less passed through his lung. And there's this . . ."

He pulled a scrawled-over piece of paper from a bag at his feet. He also pulled his half glasses out and reviewed the paper.

"A rifle consistent with this shell casing was stolen today from a gun shop. A woman saw a guy run out with it. She tried to chase him but he lost her. She described him as a white male, unknown age, blond or sandy brown hair, wearing a halibut jacket and maybe a hooded sweatshirt and a baseball cap.

"That could be anybody off any fishing boat in the North Pacific, Doggy. Who's the woman who saw him?"

"I don't know who she was. She wasn't from here. Who was the guy? Do you have any ideas? What do you think?"

"Stop asking me. I don't know what I think. How in the hell should I know who stole the rifle?"

"Were you drinking tonight?"

"No—a couple of beers."

"A couple of beers."

"I drank a lot last night."

"I know that. I already talked to Duarte. Sounds like a big night. By the way, he gave me this."

He reached into his bag and handed me my credit card.

"He said you left this at the restaurant. I think he may have been on the phone all morning. I'll call the company and tell them you might have some funny charges, if you like."

"Thanks, I'll take care of it."

Being in debt to a cop is a bad way to start off an interview. Doggy knew exactly that. He smiled a kind of mean avuncular grin.

"Listen, Cecil, I know you're not supposed to talk about your cases but it looks like someone tried to whack you tonight. What are you working on?"

"Nothing. Nothing. A stupid real-estate claim, a Workers' Comp. neck-brace thing, and a couple of piddly sexual assaults where the guys are going to plead out. Nothing to get killed over."

"You had a bunch of papers in your house about an old murder case."

"Louis Victor. That's right."

"You've got to talk to me, Cecil. I'm trying to help you. If you know anything, you should tell me. This is obviously bigger than you bargained for. No matter what it is."

"It's nothing, Doggy. It's a writing job. The old lady in the home wants to die happy. I'm going to tell her what she wants to know and then send her a bill. Doggy—you know that the Louis Victor case is already solved."

We stared at each other for a long awkward moment until we both realized that we were staring. And then we paused to see who could get out gracefully.

"Yeah, I know." Doggy smiled again. "It's just that I'm a little concerned about you, Cecil. I knew your father. I'm sorry about him. You and I don't know each other real well but I know a lot about you. I don't want you to get in trouble or hurt."

"Doggy, you don't know shit about me. . . ."

"Now, Cecil, that's not quite true," he said firmly, with the tone of a patient day-care worker. He reached into his bag and brought out a file, replaced his half glasses, and started reading.

"You are . . . let's see . . . thirty-six and you were born in Juneau. Your dad, of course, is . . . was"—he looked up with that sympathetic look that addresses my family's disappointment—"'the Judge.' Your sister's earned a good name as an attorney and now teaches at Yale. You studied music and art history at Reed College until you were thrown out. You got into drugs. The drugs weren't the problem at Reed. You got tossed for never showing up for lectures or exams."

He looked up with a cute little "fuck you" grin and kept reading.

"After Reed, in '73 you traveled in Africa and Asia, studying religion and music, and . . . I don't suppose you call it 'contemplating your navel,' do you? No. You worked for a time in the oil patch in Wyoming and on the tugs on the Inside Passage, and you traveled around the South singing in choirs—?"

Another look.

"Sacred Harp chorus. Get to the good stuff."

His voice was taking on more of a biting tone. There were no happy lines around his eyes. "The good stuff. Well, your daddy wanted you to be a lawyer, so he set you up as an investigator with the Public Defender Agency, hoping that if you carried enough briefcases for snotty little lawyers younger than you, you'd be shamed into going to law school. But you got in some trouble that involved cocaine and a small matter of suborning perjury. You did a little time— very little time—and your record was wiped clean. You moved to Sitka and played at being Sam Spade with your sister's money. You stayed sober until your daddy died, and then you played the drunken aesthete until your girlfriend left you. Now your roommate is shot in the chest and may die."

"What's the point?"

"The point is this, friend. This is real life. This is Toddy's life. I'd feel a little better about all of this if you had gotten shot, but you didn't. So go home, get drunk or fucked up any way you want. But stay out of this. What happened tonight is a real crime, Younger. There is no room for a damaged, confused rich kid roaming around fucking up this investigation."

I should have thought of some icy retort that would have shown him how cool and incisive I was. I should have said something that would have thrown the entire weight of his disdain back on him in three or four words.

"Oh, yeah? Make me."

"Get out of here, Younger. Get drunk. Get stoned. Just stay out of the way."

He walked out the door and I settled back in the chair by the window. Across the road there was a street lamp above the water and the reflection was milky white on the surface of the bay. I thought of broken bones.

Toddy lay in bed surrounded by blinking machines and tubes. His face was as white as a plaster mask. I wanted to shake him, scold him for being so lazy as to be in bed. I wanted to wrap him up and take him home to our house, the fire, the halibut, and the certainties of the encyclopedias. The nurse came in and told me to leave. I was not to have any more meetings in Todd's room and there was someone else outside to see me.

It was a nice young cop outside the room who was embarrassed about not taking my shirt at the police station. It was useless to put up much of a fuss. Even through his embarrassment he had a stiff way of asking questions that became even stiffer as Doggy passed in the hall. He slipped the shirt into a paper bag and, after stapling it closed, he thanked me. He told me to have a nice evening. I wanted to go home.

The rain was hardly noticeable as I walked down the main street past the cathedral. I turned at the Pioneer Home. My jail pants slowly became heavy and damp, my hair matted down. I had my jacket on with no shirt underneath. It seemed to be darker than usual. The street lamps were like stepping-stones of light. I walked from one to another with my head down, my hands jammed into my pockets. If someone was trying to kill me, I would be an easy shot but I didn't much care. The blood that had dried to a dark crust on the rims of my fingernails was liquid again in the rain. I could smell blood on my skin. I thought of the surf breaking in the darkness on the outer rocks, and I thought of someone trying to kill me.

On the waterfront, the bar was clogged with fishermen, hooting and telling stories. The cracked speaker on the jukebox buzzed as another Bruce Springsteen song limped out of it. It was bingo night at the Alaska Native Brotherhood Hall. A Tlingit kid was riding his tricycle at the door, skirting the edge of the sidewalk as his brother watched him. As I walked by he looked over his handlebars and whispered, "Hi, Cecil."

Down at our house the cops had finished digging the slug out of the door frame and there was yellow tape strung over the entrance. A hand-painted sign that said, "CRIME SCENE.

DO NOT ENTER" was taped to the door. Upstairs, a white linen curtain billowed out of an open window.

I thought of Peter Pan, never wanting to grow up, lifting children in their nightgowns out of open windows. The curtain, soaking in the rain, popped in the breeze once, and I thought of a white plume of air escaping a sinking ship.

FIVE

I SWEAR TO GOD, when I saw my father lying dead on the floor of the casino, with five-dollar gold pieces raining down on his chest, I thought, "That lucky son of a bitch." His skin was a pale gray against the green of the carpet. Lights were flashing, a siren throbbed, all announcing the winner of the super $100,000 jackpot. The photographer from the publicity department arrived before the paramedics. Two women with golf gloves on their lever hands eyed the machine and the money sparkling down on the dead man, and they were caught in their own swirls of calculation: randomness, inevitability, and luck. They watched and flexed their fingers into fists and then were hustled off to new machines and given complimentary tickets to the floor show. The pit boss nervously twisted his wedding ring, and a man in cowboy boots and a security uniform talked into a handheld radio.

He had died of a stroke while the slot machine came up with three gold nuggets that read "Motherlode."

The Judge was not a big fan of irony, and it probably pissed him off to die in Las Vegas. He also did not believe much in chance. At least for himself. Chance was the agent of randomness, and randomness was only visited upon those who were out of control. Thousands of defendants had stood before him over the years and in their many pleas they always said the same thing: Their lives had somehow gotten away from them. They stood before him and he looked at them clinically, without anger or blame. He looked at them as an emergency-room doctor might look at the victims of a tornado, clutching their crying babies and gesturing to their household goods strewn down the street.

"The big mistake," he used to say, sitting on a spruce stump, cradling his rifle on his lap, "is to blame nature. Nature is orderly. It is not necessarily benevolent but it has purpose. It is not God's responsibility to bring you good luck. It is your business to pack everything you need and put yourself into the way of good fortune." And then he would usually sit very quietly on his stump, blow a deer call, and wait.

By the time he was thirty the Judge knew the name of every bird he encountered on his hunting trips—both the common and the Latin names. He carried field guides in his hunting pack, one for birds and one for plants. He carried *Meditations on Hunting* but I never saw him read it. He planned out every hunting strategy by numerical navigation, using the topographical map, a compass, and a six-inch ruler he carried with him in his pouch. The first thing out of the skiff, he would sit on a stump, smoke a cigarette, and plot a course. He figured the wind, the temperature, the moisture, and the time of day in relation to the time of year. Often, he would read through his journal from the previous year to try and reconstruct a pattern. The Judge hunted by intellectual calculation. The deer were his objective and he was plotting a conquest.

The older he got, the more strategy he relied on: trying to foretell the deer's patterns and call them to a precise place at a precise time. When he was younger he had broken through the thick tangles of salmonberry and alder to get to the top of the ridge by first light. He said that he used to rush the deer on the first day of the season as if he were in rut. But by the time I was old enough to go with him he was a flirtatious hunter: gesture, feint, and unspoken intent.

I've always been a blundering hunter. The fact that I ever got a deer at all is a testimony to the fallibility of the species. The Judge said that I was good for the country because I was obviously culling the stupid genes from the pool.

I would clatter around in the brush and with each step my boots would make a loud slurp while coming out of the mud. At first the Judge would wince when hunting with me, suffering to try and make me move quietly. Then he began to plant himself on a stump and send me off to circle around and hunt back on the game trails toward him. Most often I would be moving through the woods and hear the crack of his rifle ahead of me. I would stop for a moment and, almost in time with my own breath, I would hear the next, finishing shot. I'd shoulder my rifle and walk briskly on, glad I didn't have to keep up the hunt.

Once into the clearing I would usually find a buck hung on a low limb and the Judge, with his sleeves rolled up, wiping the last of the blood off his hands with a clump of moss. He would be smoking a cigarette, and as I'd come through the opening of the brush he'd turn and ask how I did. I would tell him I'd seen some sign but didn't get off a shot. He'd look at me briefly, with that long stare, then jerk his head toward the deer and say, "Well, he won't walk to the skiff himself."

It didn't always happen that way. Once in mid-October, when I was a senior in high school, a buck turned back on his course toward the Judge and his high perch on the spruce stump. My rifle sling was frayed, and I was sitting on a fallen log trying to shorten it past the worn spot of leather. I imagine the Judge would have said I was "just half there." I was thinking of the girl who sat in front of me in physics class and how her blouse hiked up off the small of her back so that I could see the walnut dimples of her backbone disappear down into her skirt. I might have been thinking about her breath in my ear as I fiddled with the stiff leather of my sling.

When the buck snorted, my rifle leaped out of my hand and fell like a walking stick next to the tree. He was a small Sitka blacktail with spindly forked horns. His neck was thick, and he had the dark brows on his forehead that folded down neatly into the light, almost feathery, shimmer around his throat. His muscles were tight and his stance was low with a slight crouch. His eyes were dark and would have been impassive if it weren't for the bundled energy of his body. Watching him was like listening to a guitar string being tuned up higher and higher, until the anticipation of its breaking almost hurt.

I reached for my rifle, fully expecting him to explode past me into the trees, saving us both. I touched the grips, still expecting him to run. I put it to my cheek and I peered down the sights. He stood there, perhaps believing he was invisible, perhaps denying the reality of this figure, the motion of the hand, as much as I was. I wasn't sure I wanted the deer but I was certain I wanted to carry it into the clearing in front of the Judge. I pulled the trigger and the buck popped like a balloon and fell to the ground. There was not much blood and there was not much drama, but what was once muscle, bone, and movement became an empty bag.

I carried it into the clearing and the Judge looked down and said, "Well, you're going to have to eat that thick-necked bastard." And he hopped off the stump and headed for the skiff.

It had only been ten months since Las Vegas and the bluster of well-wishers and practiced mourners. My sister in her dark glasses and rumpled cotton suit, getting off the plane into the desert air, saying, "My God, it's dry. Let's get a drink." And I had one, the first in six months. My sister knew that, as she ordered me more rounds. We listened to country western music in the airport bar, and we talked about luck, gambling, and anvils falling from the sky.

These memories—of my sister, the Judge, and the blacktail deer—clung to me like a dusting of pollen when I woke up the next morning. I swung my legs over the side of the bed. I rubbed my eyes and saw the line of blood encrusted in the cuticles on my right hand. I called the hospital and asked about Todd. The nurse asked who I was and I told her that I was from the Lakeview Thoracic Trauma Center in Seattle. Her tone changed and she told me Todd was sleeping well and had stabilized overnight although his doctor was concerned about a fever developing. I thanked her and told her I would contact the doctor directly.

I called a friend who worked at the Pioneer Home and asked a couple of favors. I asked her if anyone had been to room 104 in the last two days. She said, "No one besides Mrs. Victor."

I called the airline and made my reservation to Juneau.

I called the prison to tell them I was coming to interview Alvin Hawkes.

Dickie Stein called to check in with me and to tell me that it didn't look like the D.A. was going to press his investigation my way but for me to watch myself. I said I would be watching.

I packed my duffel bag. One white shirt, socks, underwear, rubber rain shoes, two phone books, a buckskin pouch with my shaving kit, two spiral notebooks, four number-two pencils with the fat pencil-cap erasers, my handmade Gouker skinning knife with the harness leather sheath, and a microcassette tape recorder that I like to carry in my coat pocket when I'm looking for something and not sure when I'm going to find it. I thought of bringing a bottle of Wild Turkey, but didn't. Drinking whiskey out of the bottle when someone is trying to kill you is probably not a good idea unless they are matching you drink for drink.

I made a sandwich out of Todd's halibut. I mixed it with mayonnaise and chopped onions. I spread it on black bread and drank a glass of tomato juice. As I ate, I looked at the bookshelf where Todd kept his series of picture books that he had agreed to buy after speaking for a half hour to a friendly salesman. Even though we never paid for them, we still received the books along with notices from collection agencies. There was a Richie Rich comic book stuck as a bookmark into a thin volume with a painting of a ship on the cover. I drank a beer, then a shot of bourbon.

Todd's father called from a logging camp west of Ketchikan. He was drunker than I was, and crying. He wanted to know how much the medical bills would be. The police had contacted him by phone and asked about Todd's relationship to me and asked about drugs and guns. He wanted to know what was going on.

I told him that I would take care of the bills and he could come up and visit when he got out of the woods. He said he would like to visit but his boss was riding him hard. He would see if he could make it by plane sometime in the next week. He asked why someone had shot Todd. I told him I didn't know. Then he threatened to cut my nuts off if I had anything to do with it. I thanked him and hung up.

I called a local junkie who drives a cab and owes me a lifetime of free rides to the airport and told him when my flight was.

The bourbon and the beer were working softly at the edge of my unhappiness. I suppose a narcotic would have been more direct, especially with the added thrill of my imminent murder. Narcotics work great but not if you have a plane to catch. I thought of having another drink. I was drunk enough to be stupid but not drunk enough to be helpless. These are tough decisions.

The junkie took me across the bridge to the airport. He was nervous about doing a freebie for me and thought for sure every passing car would know the meter wasn't running. He mumbled something about Todd and asked me for a loan. I hinted around for a touch of dope but he was spooky and I was uncertain.

Bloom was standing at the security gate. I went into the bathroom.

My unhappiness was becoming more and more mysterious as I walked up to Bloom at the gate. Before my bag even went through the scanner he took it and pawed through it. He took out my hunting knife.

"This is a weapon, Younger. You can't have this in the cabin with you."

"So?"

"So you'll have to check it as luggage."

I watched the attendant tag my knife, then I watched it move past the rubber curtain on the conveyor belt. It was small and vulnerable, and I hoped it would be all right, but in fact I never saw it again. A Gouker skinning knife is the finest knife a man can own, and someone else recognized that, too.

Bloom needed to frisk me and he backed me up against the glass partition of the security area and ran his hands under my coat and down my pants. I was thinking of Miles Davis and trying to remember one of the riffs in "Funny Valentine." Bloom's hands felt damp and soft as they kneaded the muscles down to the small of my back.

"How's someone like you stay in shape, Younger?"

"Hard work, clean living, and a nice smile."

He stood up suddenly and I thanked him. He patted me once on the back as I went out through the doors of the terminal. I looked around and told him to have a nice day.

The plane was late in taking off and they served champagne. The stewardess had an appropriate perky smile but dark eyes that looked like holes in a painting. Our fingertips brushed slightly as I took the plastic cup of champagne from her hands.

Just after we took off, the jet banked steeply to the east and we flew back over the airport. I looked down on my little toy town. Toy post office and windup trucks. I thought about the book from the woman who used to love me sitting on the bench of the Pioneer Home. I could see my house with the blue flower boxes hanging over the water on the second floor. I thought I saw someone pedaling a bike with thick tires and a large basket past my front door.

I didn't notice I was crying until a stewardess came by and gave me a tissue to blow my nose in. Her arm and wrist were slender and they formed a pretty arch, like the limb of a fruit tree, as she poked the tissue into my clenched fist. She didn't look at my eyes. It was a perfect gesture, an expression of indifference and concern, which is the most a drunk can ask for.

SIX

THE STATE SPARED no expense on razor ribbon wire when they decided to beef up security around the Lemon Creek Correctional Institution. Rounding the last curve, it looks like you're driving up on the Maginot Line. The prison is tucked back up a newly glaciated valley on the banks of Lemon Creek. There are scrubby spruce and alder trees on both sides of the creek, and I always have the feeling the glacier is just over my shoulder. The water of the creek is silty, almost opaque. The current is slow as the creek begins to meander at sea level toward the salt water of Gastineau Channel. It flows past the prison and down past several trailer parks. There used to be wrecked cars on the shores to hold the banks in place. In a few of the ragged alders kids from the trailer parks had tried to hang rope swings from the skinny limbs until the creek sucked the trees, root systems and all, into the slow current. One rope fluttered in the dirty water. The children had given up trying to swing over the creek and were inside their trailers watching TV.

From the exercise yard a prisoner could see eagles circling the garbage on the creek bank. Once when I was there

I saw a raven hopping outside the fence line with a waxed-paper bag of french fries dripping from his beak. Raven who stole light from the darkness.

I was prepared for the strip search inside the visitors' decompression lockup. They knew me by my first name, and they took the time to look into "my third eye," as the grinning security guard referred to it. It's an easy procedure, kind of like walk-in surgery. There are no pen lights or tongue depressors. They just ask you to take your clothes off and squat and cough as hard as you can and then they see if anything falls out. The guard was nice about it. Maybe it was because he knew me.

I put my clothes back on and clipped a visitor's tag onto my shirt. All I had was my 3-by-5 spiral notebook and a pencil; everything else was in a locker. I stood in the sealed passageway to the visitors' interview rooms. One wall was covered with bulletproof one-way reflective glass. I checked my hair and smiled. The buzzer sounded and then I heard the clunk of a heavy lock giving way. A voice from a speaker informed me, "We'll bring Hawkes up to room four, Cecil."

The door swung open. Down a hall were several locked doors with bulletproof windows. A young guard with an empty holster stood beside an open door. "Hawkes will be right up."

I walked past the interview rooms. In one, a woman had her head down on the table, resting her forehead on her hands, and an Eskimo man was banging his palms on the tabletop.

I walked into room four. It was about six feet by ten feet and at the far end was another door with a window that looked out on to the main prison hallway, which led from the dorm rooms to the stairwell that goes to the shop. Men

walked past slowly as if ambling down to the corner for a
pack of smokes. Some were wearing prison blues; others,
white T-shirts. All of them looked in at me and several of
them waved. One held up a slip of paper on which he had
written, "APPEAL?" I shrugged, holding my hands out in a
gesture of helplessness.

After a few minutes a guard stood at the window holding a
young man by the arm. He unlocked the door and led the
man in. Then he pointed to the phone on my left and said,
"Dial zero when you're done, Cecil." I thanked him and he
left, locking the door behind him.

The door snapped shut with a sudden authority, making
me wince. I thought of the eagle circling above the sky blue
ice of the glacier, I thought of the raven hopping on the curb
with the red thread on his leg, far away from here, very far.

Alvin Hawkes came into the room and sat across
the table. His hands were crossed in front of him. He was
only a wiry five foot six or seven. He wore wire-rimmed
reading glasses. He had the stubble of a recently shaved
head and the purple bruises of homemade tattoos on the
backs of his hands. His left hand had a symbol for infinity on
it and the word "GODS" was written across the knuckles of
the right.

He looked at me, squinting and wrinkling his nose.
Either he was curious or he thought something I was wearing would be good to eat. Hawkes had small blue eyes that
were deeply set. His jaw muscles flexed as I began to talk.

"My name is Cecil Younger. I'm a private detective. I've
been hired by Louis Victor's mother to find out why you
killed her son."

Now his smile became broad as if it were clear that
everything was funny, including me. He began to chuckle

and then laugh. It was a laugh you heard a lot in jail. It sounded like rocks clattering far back in a cave.

"It was nice of you to come see me." He stood up and extended his hand. "Why don't you dial zero, I've got to go to the library."

"You won't talk to me?"

"It doesn't show much respect, Mr. Younger, to come here and start talking to me about a killing. A killing I have been suspected of committing, arrested for, convicted for, and am now serving a sentence for. Have you talked to my lawyer?"

"No—would that make a difference?"

"Well. There it is." And he held his hands palms up with his elbows pressed tightly to his sides. He was smiling. "There it is."

"I'm sorry. I don't follow you."

"Would it make a difference? That's a good question . . . to talk to my lawyer, I mean. I don't think it would. Talking to lawyers has never made a difference as far as I can tell." He sat back down. "What does she want to know?"

"Why did you kill her son?"

"She doesn't know? She really doesn't know?" He leaned back and put one elbow up on the back of his chair.

"There was a time when my lawyers wanted to pursue . . . I don't know what you'd call it—a gambit—I don't know—a strategy, to make the cops believe that I was . . . unstable— emotionally. They believed that I could gain some advantage. Sentencing consideration. You can see that backfired." He smiled broadly and gestured around the cell like a character actor in a drawing-room comedy. He paused briefly, then he leaned forward and lowered his voice.

"I played along with them because I got advice, scientific advice, that I should exercise restraint and I should be patient with what the lawyers had to say." For the first time he looked at me directly and his stare didn't waver. "I knew you were coming," he said deliberately.

"How did you know?"

He smiled sweetly again, as if he were worried about me.

"I was informed. I understand now that I should tell you the whole truth."

I was a little uncomfortable with his choice of words. "What is the whole truth?"

"Do you know much about science? Have you ever heard of alpha wave ionizers?"

"No." I opened my notebook and held my pencil attentively: the scribe.

"Well, you can read about them. I've read about them a lot. You know, the earth generates energy. Well, most of it comes from the sun, but that's different, that is solar energy, but the earth generates its own from the dense atmosphere that gathers in the north. You are familiar with the aurora borealis? The energy that I'm speaking of is similar, yet it takes the form of alpha wave particles." He took my notebook and drew a squiggle on my pad. "Where do you think radio waves go? TV? All of the taxi cabs have radios. We are surrounded by wave particles; it's like we're swimming in them, but you can't hear them or see them. If you said you could you'd be crazy. That's because they aren't organic, that's because they don't come from the earth itself."

He leaned forward and spoke slowly so I would have time to understand this next: "Now this is true. Everybody is born with the ability to receive the earth's transmissions, but most people can't. The further north you go, the better your ability to receive. The earth concentrates the waves near the pole."

I hadn't started writing and he was looking at my pad. I quickly wrote the date and then the words, "True . . . concentrated transmissions."

"This is the truth. I know it may be hard for you to accept but something extraordinary has happened to me. There is a thin flap of membrane that anyone can open up by concentration. You have it. Everybody has it." He pointed to my ear. "But to open it you must have intense powers of concentration. I have opened that flap. I am free to receive."

"Who is speaking to you?"

"Now, put yourself in my place. I mean, you start hearing voices. That's crazy, right? So you have to start sorting it out. That confused me for a long time. I was getting a lot of signals; there are so many signals, many voices, if you will. Think about it: tree voices, cloud voices, fish voices. I was getting them all." He leaned back. "It was weird." Then he lowered his voice to almost a whisper. "It takes concentration to be able to tune them out, but that is the Devil for you. That's the Devil for you, because the key to remember is . . . don't tune them out. Tune them *in*."

His voice was quavering. He leaned forward. "You can actually tune them in all together and get one strong signal, one incredibly strong signal."

He stopped and in an instant became aware of himself and sat back, a little embarrassed. Where at first he was coy he was now taut, staring like a bear assessing a photographer. At the same time he couldn't shed that film of self-awareness. There was something ironic about him, in his gestures, the fake professorial diction, as if he were absorbed by his own act, unable to break out of character.

"I knew the voices were the truth. But as weird as it was, I had to prove it to other people."

He reached into his pockets and took out two small pieces of tinfoil. He formed them with his thumbs until they were shaped like cups. Then he put the cups over his ears. He paused and rolled his eyes up to the ceiling, listened for a moment, nodded as if confirming something he had every confidence in and then smiled.

"I've now blocked the transmissions; I can't hear a thing. I can do this a hundred times and a hundred times the voices stop. These are verifiable and reproducible results. This is scientific. It's not just my word for it. There has to be a physical basis for the voices or how else could the foil stop them?"

A white man with a braided beard walked by on the prison side of the glass and made a face by pulling out his cheeks with his forefingers and waggling his tongue around. I waved and he walked on.

"Funny? I know." Hawkes smiled confidently. "Everyone thinks it's funny but it won't be so funny when I harness the full potential of these waves."

"Are you seeing a doctor in here, Alvin? Someone you can tell about these voices?"

He fished into his shirt pocket for a can of snoose, tapped the lid twice with his fingertips, twisted the lid off, and took a two-finger dip of tobacco. "Don't need a doctor. The reason I'm the way I am is I have terrific control. This is true. I know I'm different from everybody else here and they know it, too." As he said the word "they," he pointed his thumb toward the ceiling, leaving a question in my mind as to who "they" referred to.

"Listen, Alvin, I know you've been asked this already, but are you sorry for killing Louis Victor? Thinking about it, does it make you sad?"

He leaned forward again. He had the shadow of a scar above his left cheek. His chest was shiny and showed a dark stubble and one razor nick above the top button of his shirt. He squinted at me as if he were trying to read something written on the tip of my nose.

"I didn't kill Louis Victor," he wheezed. "God killed him. God reached up through the earth and killed him."

"Are you an agent of God, Alvin?"

"We're all agents of God, some of us are just more attentive."

"Did God tell you to kill Louis Victor?"

"No, God told everything on earth to kill him, and I just happened to be listening."

He leaned back in his chair and took off his glasses with a professorial gesture. "Do you remember in the story of Jonah when God directs the worm to eat the roots of the fig tree that was shading Jonah out in front of the temple? That was just a fable, he was really directing the whole earth to teach Jonah a lesson. You can't really blame it all on the worm. I am a worm, you are a worm, and all of the guards and lawyers are, too. It's true, you see. When I was younger I was confused by that, but not now. Worms. I used to be dirty and I was lazy. I couldn't pay attention to what was being said. I was covered with bacteria. Bacteria breeds in body hair. I used to have lots of hair and my stepfather used to whip me for having my hair too long. He was being like the worm, moving and sort of swimming in the earth surrounded by God."

"Who killed Louis Victor, Alvin?"

"You mean who actually stopped the electrical workings of his brain?"

"Yes."

Hawkes looked down. I could hear him flicking his thumbnail under the table. He closed his eyes.

"You know, before I gained so much control I was very sinful. I did terrible things."

"What did you do, Alvin?"

He was forcing his eyes shut now, squeezing them shut, painfully tight, as if trying to keep out any trace of light. Then he covered his eyes with his fists. He was breathing hard, his chest heaving.

"I used bad language. I had sex with dirty girls whose whole bodies stank with sin. I even had the clap. I was mean to my mother and to my grandmother. I was mean to children in school. God doesn't like that. God doesn't like that. But when I first started to hear the voices they told me that I was forgiven."

"Did God forgive you for killing Louis?"

His body appeared to be rigid, and I could see sweat soaking through the armpits of his prison blues.

"Louis was going to kill me. He was going to turn into a bear and eat me. Bears and humans eat the same kinds of food. Louis was going to eat me, and I had to feed him to the bear first. I was very, very confused. I was hearing crazy things. I thought I was God. That couldn't be true, could it? That's just crazy, after all of the . . . sinful things I had done. That couldn't be true, could it?"

He looked at me with a frantic questioning expression, eyes darting back and forth.

"Finally, I couldn't keep it in, and I had to tell Louis about the voices and about what kinds of things they were saying. He started yelling at me. He said he had to get rid of me. That's what he said—get rid of me. Not fire me or let me go, but get rid of me. His son and daughter were on the boat

71

and he said that he was going to sleep with them. I remember him with a gun in his hand. I knew he was going to kill me."

Hawkes stood up. His voice was urgent and his eyes were focused on the blank space next to the door.

"I walked toward him as he was bending down by the bed. He stood up and hit me." Hawkes crouched in a wrestler's stance, still staring at the space in front of the door. "I remember charging him and we tumbled out the door. I was thrown back inside, and I remember him coming at me with a splitting maul."

He covered his ears, and shook his head slowly and intently as if he were easing into a trance. "I don't remember any more, the voices won't let me remember any more. All they say is crazy stuff. They say I'm a thunder storm. I'm a hurricane. That I could flatten this prison. The voices say that I'm stronger than God. That's crazy. How could God create something stronger than himself?"

He sat down, one hand flat on the table. He flicked his thumbnail. He focused on it.

"The only thing I know is the membrane receiver popped open and then shut and then opened again when I talked to the cops. I remember it clearly, the pop in my inner ear. I remember flying on a helicopter. I remember sitting in a room like this with the troopers. I remember talking to the lawyers. But something won't let me remember anything about killing Louis."

"Do you remember anything at all about that day?"

"Only that it was windy. That night there were two boats in the harbor, Louis's and a troller. Louis's boat had to reset its anchor because of the wind. Louis was angry because his son had anchored so close to the beach."

"Anything else?"

"Only crazy stuff."

"Tell me."

"I thought that Louis was a bear and he was going to kill me. And that his children were half-bear, half-human and they wanted me to kill him so they could eat him. The voices said that this would please God.

"I know that this is crazy stuff. I know it was only because I was dirty then and the bacteria in my hair was screwing up all of the signals. You see it's very complicated."

"Where did you see his kids?"

"I never saw them. The troopers told me they were afraid to come to the beach."

I phoned the guard station and I told them I was done. I knew that they would take their time. I folded up my notebook and stood up as if I were going to take a short walk around the room. I leaned up against the visitors' door and Hawkes leaned against the prison door.

"What do you think, Alvin? You angry that you're in here?"

"It doesn't matter much. I'm different from everyone else." He stood up and looked out to the prison side of the door. "You ever pulled down a barn?"

"A barn? No, no, I haven't."

"I used to do that for a job back in Illinois. Lots of these old barns have to come down. You know the old wooden ones? I was the rat man. They called me the 'rat man' anyway because my job was to cut away at the beams and the supports. I'd weaken the whole building. Just nibble away at it with my saw and then set the chain to a center support and pull it down. I'd stand there and watch and listen, just before the last pull. I'd make sure everyone was out. I'd look around, you know, and it was really quiet. The sun came through the cracks in the wood and there were webs across the doors and stuff. It was as quiet and spooky as the inside of my head. Then they'd pull it down.

"I'd stand near the door and the air would blast past me, like a wind, you know. It smelled like dust and bird shit and dry hay. I could hear the nails screaming, being wrenched out of the wood, and timbers breaking. I'd stand there and listen and smell . . . and then it was flat. It was gone.

"I don't know . . . prison's not so bad. You know what I mean?"

He picked up his glasses from the table. The buzzer sounded on Alvin's side of the room, and a guard stood on the other side of the window. Alvin fished in his pockets to make sure he had his tinfoil cups and he nodded a good-bye.

"Good luck," I said, and he smiled at me, as if there were something ironic about the expression.

SEVEN

IT'S NOT HARD to find people in Juneau. The suspects are drinking in bars on one side of the street and their lawyers are drinking on the other. I was in the North Pole Bar and I would bet fully half the clientele in the North Pole that night were in violation of the terms of their releases. Some were keeping a low profile, hunched over their drinks like bulldogs over their last bits of food. Emanuel Marco wasn't keeping a low profile. He was wearing his broad-brimmed hat, and as he walked he was weaving like a dancing bear. He was wearing a full-length leather coat and I knew that he was carrying a gun in the deep inside pocket and had a Balinese throwing knife tucked into his boot. Corny, but I think Emanuel thought it added to his aura as a-man-not-to-be-taken-lightly.

"It was just a voice on the fucking phone, man. It rang here, man said he was trying to get me since nine this morning. Some guy asking what it would take to have you killed. *You*, man, Cecil fucking Younger."

This struck him as incredibly funny. He wheezed out a tobacco-breath laugh that ended in a mucus gag and a swallow. Then he tried to focus on me.

"He must have had the wrong guy. I mean, first of all, you're nowhere near important enough to have killed. I mean, who in the fuck is going to pay the five grand it takes to have you whacked? We were just sitting around trying to figure it out, Cecil. You don't know anyone important. All of your enemies are either cops or scumbags. The cops can do you anytime they want, and the scumbags can't afford to."

A round of laughter went up around the bar. The bartender, chuckling, continued to wipe the bar with a damp rag.

"I feel safer all the time."

"I wouldn't worry about it, man. It was somebody just jerking me off. Let me get you a drink."

He turned his back on me and shouted down the bar at the bartender, who was now leaning across the counter under the TV set trying to talk to a blond lady who was crying and stirring her drink with her finger.

The North Pole is a room for serious drinking. It is long and narrow with a high ceiling that holds the thick smoke above the patrons like a summer fog. There is a mirror and a lineup of bottles. There are no stuffed animal heads or pictures of ships foundering on reefs. There is one beer company sign that has shimmering lights behind a scene of a hunter getting ready to shoot a stag just cresting a hill. The only artifact of honor is in the center above the bottles: an eight-inch basketball trophy. The inscription is tarnished; none of the bartenders know who won it or when. The single leather booth near the bathroom door has been slashed across the bottom so that anyone sitting there sinks awkwardly into the stuffing. The bathrooms are in the rear, and the closer you get to them, the stronger the smell of the round deodorant bricks that are in the bottoms of the urinals. I woke up in one of the bathrooms once in broad daylight and saw some kind of tobacco-colored stalactites hanging from the ceiling. The North Pole doesn't serve mineral water, and the bartenders don't give out information about any of the patrons to outsiders unless under subpoena.

Seated next to the blond woman was a woman with raven black hair. She was wearing a blue North Pole Bar windbreaker. Her head rested on the bar and her arms were folded over her head. She held a lighted cigarette in one hand, a five-dollar bill wadded in the other. She had the hiccups. The bartender took a slice of lemon and doused it with bitters and then a pinch of salt. He placed it in front of her.

"Lucille? Eat this."

She looked up at him in confusion as if he were standing at her door at four in the morning. Without a glimmer of recognition, she ate the lemon. "Fuck it," she said. She took a deep breath and sighted down her cigarette, then stubbed it out.

The key to life in the North Pole was to avoid the sunlight and to survive until the night crowd came in. Once that happened anything was possible.

Over in the corner nearest to Lucille was the bar's only icon. It was a small religious painting. One of the old owners of the bar had been Russian Orthodox and he had put a Russian icon in there but it caused such a stir that the bishop himself came down to see that it was taken out. The owner then found a picture in a library book and ordered a copy of it for the far end of the bar. It was embossed and then mounted behind unbreakable glass and bolted to the wall underneath the hot dog rotisserie. There were scratches on the glass but no writing. The bishop heard about the new image but understood it was a page torn from a book and as long as it wasn't really an icon he couldn't muster the energy to go down to the bar again. Besides, he had heard the painting was by an Italian.

It was a little reproduction of the Crucifixion by Anatello da Messina. I had once watched it for the better part of a day, and it was one of the best reasons to drink in this bar. Grünewald had painted the torture of the Crucifixion and the ecstasy of the Resurrection in two separate paintings, but Messina's Christ was caught in the middle: tired, with his head to one side, beautiful and expectant . . . but sad nonetheless. The hills beyond Golgotha were sprinkled with the sizzling green light of the olive trees and the sky was the milky blue of an ascending morning. Why would anyone want to leave such an earth?

The ceiling of the bar was painted black yet the smoke still seemed to stain it. The cushions on the stools were red leather and the electric beer sign illuminated the patrons' skin like a lamp designed to kill bugs. Lucille sat with her head slumped down in front of the Messina, with the five-dollar bill still wadded up in her hand. And she still had the hiccups.

"Fuck it . . . fuck it."

Emanuel Marco put the bourbon and water on the bar in front of me. I looked at my watch and it was 2:30 P.M.

"So why in the fuck would somebody want to kill you?"

"Don't know. Maybe somebody trying to get back at my old man."

"They sure as fuck wouldn't kill you if they wanted to hurt *his* feelings."

Again, the snot-sucking laugh. Marco was the kind of guy

I hoped wouldn't grow on me. "Hey, I heard about the Judge. I'm sorry, man." The laugh became a stifled smirk.

"What do you know about Louis Victor?"

Emanuel sighted an imaginary rifle down the bar. "Man, he was the best. 'Boom.' The Indian motherfucker could shoot. Best I ever saw. Best my old man ever saw. He used a 45–70. An old army round. I heard that crazy guy who killed him was one huge motherfucker. Huge. Thought he was a bear. Revenging all the lost souls of his brother bears or some shit like that. Anyway, you'd have to be awful big and awful crazy to take on Louis Victor."

"Victor ever get in trouble with the cops?"

"Nothing serious, you know. Maybe assault, DWI, but shit, nothing serious. Nothing dangerous. He was clean with the Fish and Game cops. Hunting was his life, man; he couldn't afford to lose his license. I did hear that he was in some trouble when he lived up in Stellar."

"What kind?"

"I don't know. Like I said, nothing big. Blew over quick and it didn't follow him down here."

"What are his kids like?"

"Mousy. More likable than Louis maybe. You know, normal. Lance can shoot, too. He's really into guns. But he didn't want to get his hands dirty with work, like his old man did."

"You know anything about his friend Walt Robbins?"

"All I heard is the same old shit. People say that Robbins was fucking Louis's old lady when they lived up in Stellar. Robbins is a hell of a hunter, too. He wanted to go into business here in Southeastern but couldn't get the permit. I heard Louis had some pull with the game board and made sure that Robbins couldn't get a guide's permit. Why sweat the competition?"

"What caliber of gun did Robbins use?"

"Fuck, I don't know."

"You recognize the voice that talked to you on the phone this morning?"

"Naw, man, I told you—somebody just jerking me off. The voice was all husky and fake-like. It was one of my friends trying to hose me. Hey, don't worry about it, bud. It's pretty funny if you think about it."

I put five dollars on the bar, told the bartender to put it toward Lucille's cab fare, and headed across the street to see what the ruling class thought was funny. Emanuel was doing his dancing-bear routine as I left, his arms around two embarrassed tourist ladies who had obviously gotten directions to the wrong bar.

The rain had stopped and I could see the near slopes of the mountains that press in on Juneau. Juneau was built on a gold strike around the turn of the century, and the old downtown area still has the feel of a mining town. There are narrow streets and old frame houses that have the lines of Victorian affluence. The whole town clings to the side of the mountains. Of course, out on the highway there are malls and efficiently designed homes built around landscaped woods to accommodate the government workers who live in the capital city. The old downtown area is blooming with international cuisine and espresso shops. But still, down here late at night, you can hear the ore trucks that used to rumble on the planked streets. And sometimes you can hear the laughter of the Norwegian miners coming from the half-opened windows along with the practiced cooing of their whores.

The hotel across the street from the North Pole has been restored to a condition that people like to believe is authentic turn-of-the-century. There are thick carpets and English "antiques" and leaded-glass insets in some of the doors. The bar off the lobby is a power meeting place, where people who make deals and people who want to be perceived as deal makers like to drink. They definitely do serve mineral water at the bar, and the bartenders hug each other when they change shift. The jukebox has George Winston and Billie Holiday, featured but always low and in the background.

I sat at a corner table—oak veneer, with a blue hurricane lamp in the center. I ordered Maker's Mark and water and waited for someone to come in who would be of some use to me.

Stellar. I'd been looking for a reason to go to Stellar for about six months. Two people who I wanted to see were now in Stellar. So I told myself that I might be able to find something there to explain the relationship between Louis Victor and Walter Robbins.

Edward was in Stellar. At least that's what I'd heard. Edward and I had been friends in high school. He is Yupik Eskimo, from Stellar originally. He had gone to the Indian boarding school in Sitka but had gotten thrown out and come to Juneau to live with his uncle who worked in the legislature. We'd hunted together every fall. We'd meet on the docks in Juneau and load our gear into a skiff and make the crossing over to the islands off the mainland. We'd pack tarps and a tent, but often we'd move into different cabins scattered around on the homesteads or on mining claims.

We also packed whiskey. We sat in front of a rusted-out barrel stove blowing on the wet wood, passing the bottle back and forth. I think of: whiskey and drying wool, the water-stained wood in the corner of the cabin, the galvanized buckets on stumps holding the dishwater, the light smell of the kerosene lantern. With our rifles unloaded and slung over nails in the corner above the stove, we passed the bottle back and forth, talking about animals. As the bottle got lighter our gestures became wilder, our eyes widened and we imagined we were expanding into our own stories. The animals and the words combined and filled the cabin.

There is always a time when drinking and telling stories that the words begin to dissolve into vague discontent. Sentiment and romance for me . . . anger and history for Edward. Edward's speech was a strong staccato when he was sober: musical and percussive. But as he got drunker he would affect the slurred diction of a hopped-up jazz musician. Lying in the bunk, we watched the phosphorescence that glowed on the wet alder wood. The fire sputtered and Edward smoked a cigarette, stretched out in his flannel sleeping bag.

"You don't know shit about hunting. White men hunt like they're looking for a job. Get it? Salmon come up the rivers, deer come down in winter. You think it's like keeping an appointment. You work hard and all that shit, and buy expensive tools . . . you think you're pretty good."

He tried to sit up straight and I heard his elbows knocking against the planks of the bunk. "My brothers are hunters, man. Coldest place in the world. Cold . . . big . . . sooo big. You need your luck and, I don't know . . . stealth maybe. My brothers know about luck . . . all of their senses go out into the air. They move through it like wind. They never say anything bad about the bear, or the moose. They keep their luck good. Warm blood out there somewhere, like everything can smell it. They know things about the bears, bears they don't even see yet. Attention, you got to pay attention, and you take care of your luck. You don't just bump into the motherfuckers no matter how hard you work."

He lay back down, banging his head hard against his bunk, his eyes closed, bottle cradled in his arms. He was sick with bad luck, with sweat running down his neck, the wet wood in the stove hissing and popping with smoky flames.

As a private investigator I'm pretty much doomed to hunting by industry: checking records, going through files, interviewing every witness, putting myself in position for the information to come to me. But sometimes I like to fantasize about stealth, to try and understand the thoughts of my prey by smelling the air that he breathes and feeling the ground that he walks on. It's a fantasy, like I say, and it's impossible to maintain when I'm drunk. When I'm drunk my senses are blurred by vanity and pity. The perfume of the beautiful blonde.

There in the cabin we drank out of the Jack Daniel's bottle until we went to sleep. Edward reached for the bottle and toasted the air. He said his teachers at the boarding school really wanted him to be a drunk. He didn't know why but he knew it was true. He said it wasn't fair getting thrown out for doing what they wanted.

After I left college I wanted to learn something. I thought if I just filled my head with facts about music and sacred art, all the scary stuff I suspected about myself would be squeezed out, and my head and heart would lighten. Of course it didn't work, and I knew it wasn't working all the time I stood by the side of a road in north Africa with my thumb out, reed flutes and books by Henry Miller in my pack. I just ended up with more embarrassing stuff to cart around.

Edward went to college in Kansas and then went back to his village to try and live a life his grandfather would understand. He ended up on the North Slope, working in the kitchen making doughnuts for the work crews and drinking bourbon in the corner of the pantry. He didn't get in trouble. His white bosses said it was just his disease. I heard a rumor he was turning it around and giving his disease back. I had heard he was sober.

Fuck it.

There were six people in the downstairs section of the bar. I read the paper and had several more cups of coffee. It was about 5:30. Soon the predinner crowd would be ambling in: healthy young professionals, looking good in their wool slacks and fleece jackets. It was a good bar for finding defense attorneys.

I compromised between my dream state and stealth and ordered another bourbon . . . but in my coffee. Soon I would go back to just bourbon because it would be too late for coffee.

Sy Brown made his entrance, in a raw silk sports jacket with narrow lapels and a thin red tie. He stood framed by the lintel and the doorjamb, scanning the crowd. He studied each person in the bar, and he tugged on his walrus mustache. His dark eyes paused at the woman in the blue blazer and white satin blouse, then they drifted to me. Our eyes met, then he went back to the woman. He studied her as he walked toward my table. He didn't take his eyes off her as he sat down across from me. She hunted in her purse for a lighter. She wore a pearl necklace and had a pleasing shadow between her breasts.

"You need permission from me to talk to my client, Younger."

"You did such a great job for him. He just raved."

"I bet."

"Would you have given me permission?"

"No."

"So buy me a drink and tell me why you had De De Robbins whacked."

"Not funny, Younger. I've been through this shit."

He twisted around in his chair and looked at me for the first time in our conversation. "Christ, why don't you get something to wear. You always look so damn raggedy."

He sat up straight and brushed off the shoulders of his jacket as if my clothes were giving off airborne spores. Then he raised his left hand and, unbelievably, snapped his fingers for the waitress. Then he sat back.

"De De Robbins drowned herself. Why in the hell would I want her dead? She was the only one who saw the fight on the beach. She *was* my self-defense case."

"How about the Victor kids out on the boat?"

"They were down below at the time. They never heard or saw a thing until the next day when they found out that Louis was missing."

"What about Walt Robbins?"

"De De Robbins told the grand jury they had dinner, and

then the old man had a few drinks. He went below to sleep and didn't come to until the morning."

"What do you know about Louis and Walt's relationship? Did they get along?"

"Christ, you're really boring. Haven't you thought of going to law school instead of fooling around with this sleuthing business? Don't you ever think of your father?"

"Constantly. Tell me about Louis."

"Okay. He was an Alaskan stereotype—strong, proud Tlingit man, good with a gun, good finding the game. When we were looking at a self-defense claim we did a thorough check on him. He wasn't a fighter. It's like that with a lot of big guys, you know, big enough not to have to fight. There was only one case he was involved in up in Stellar. It was an alcohol-related something or another. Maybe a domestic assault, maybe a sex thing, but we had a hard time getting our hands on any of the records because they were sealed by the court to protect their confidentiality. There was some scuttlebutt that it had to do with Robbins and his relationship with Emma Victor."

"So his best friend sleeps with his wife and he beats her up for it. Was there ever a criminal case?"

"I didn't say that he beat his wife. But anyway he skated: counseling, alcohol program, and a year's probation. Nothing that half the guys up there haven't been through. Louis quit drinking after that. He'd been dry for the last ten years. People said that he was a perfect gentleman, never a harsh word. No incidents.

"Of course, none of that helped us to make our case. Here we had a man who, by all accounts, had led a good life with only one minor transgression, and he had made serious amends for that."

"Serious?"

"He quit drinking. You know anybody who's quit drinking lately?"

The waitress brought us one bourbon and water and one imported beer and a fake Waterford glass. Sy tilted the glass and poured the beer gently.

"What about Walt Robbins?"

"He was supposed to be like an uncle to the kids. They had some falling out, I guess."

"What did they do up in Stellar?"

"I guess Louis liked the tundra in the summer. The family had a fish camp, and I heard he had a love interest."

"Walt Robbins and Mrs. Victor?"

"Pay attention, Younger. It was Louis had a squeeze. That's what I heard."

"How'd Robbins react to all this?"

"Christ, you're not going to run the 'jealous lover murders the husband' routine, are you? There's nothing to tie him to it. His daughter places him down below, asleep in his berth all night."

"And she is dead."

"Fuck, Younger, grow up. If she had anything to say, don't you think she would have told it to the D.A. or the grand jury?"

"You ever turn your father in for murder, Sy?"

"No. Listen, why is your sister still teaching in New Haven? She's a great lawyer. She could be making some serious money."

"No doubt. How did Alvin Hawkes get a job with Louis?"

"He's a distant relative of someone's. I think he might even have been related to Robbins. How's that help your theory?"

"I read Hawkes's record. Clean except for those couple of drug things. Did anyone suspect that he had mental problems in his past?"

"Hell, the state still doesn't think he's got any problems. But he had no record of problems before. His mom said he was 'troubled.' Isn't that what all the relatives tell reporters after someone's gone to jail? You saw him. What do you think, is he faking it?"

"Everybody's faking it, Sy. How come you didn't get him off? Wasn't there enough around to at least stir up a little reasonable doubt?"

"Hey, listen, Younger, these were bad facts. I've got a fruitcake who just fed his boss to the bears, for Christsakes! What do you think, your big-shot sister could have worked with those facts?"

"Don't be so defensive, man. So Hawkes's family thinks they'll give their troubled boy the fresh-air treatment, and a job in Alaska is all that he needs to make a man out of him. He draws a real man for a boss, flips out, and he *thinks* he killed him. He goes to jail and the day before the trial the only witness who can help him at all gets whacked."

"Commits suicide."

"What else you know about De De Robbins?"

"Not much but I'll show you what I got."

"If she killed herself, why was she trying so hard to climb up out of the water?"

"I don't know what was going through her mind. Maybe the water was colder than she expected. Maybe she changed her mind."

"Why didn't she swim over to the ladder on the dock?"

"Don't start in on this . . . please. The experts say that

lots of suicides do unpredictable stuff. It's reflexive. Only some part of them wants to rescue themselves."

"The subconscious cavalry."

"I heard that someone got shot in Sitka last night."

"Yeah."

"I heard it was your roommate. Why in the hell aren't you working on that case instead of digging up dead college girls?"

"Pay's better. Listen, I want pictures from De De's autopsy, and I need a list of phone numbers and any travel records you've got. I'm going up to Stellar tomorrow. You going to be in early?"

"You going to see your old sweetie up there? She was a very nice-looking lady. I don't know why you had to treat her like such a piece of shit."

"I know you're just trying to spare my feelings but you don't have to refer to her in the past tense around me, Sy. I want anything you've got on the Victors or on Walt or De De Robbins. And I'll be by early tomorrow."

"Whatever. I might not be in until late."

"Then your office will be a mess when you do get in."

He spread his hands out and shrugged his shoulders. The woman with the blue blazer was drumming her fingers on the bar and studying the casing on the Taiwanese oak bar clock. Sy pushed away from our table.

"See ya."

He walked over to the woman and as I was on my way to the door I heard him ask her if he hadn't seen her in one of the local theater productions, telling her she was terrific before she could answer.

I had a cheap room upstairs. Cheap because it faced the

street and the bathroom was down the hall. The carpets smelled like mildew and cigarette smoke. No phone, no TV, but lots of cute fake antiques and a sink that didn't work just like it didn't work during the days of '98.

I walked up the stairs. In the shadows of the first landing a young couple was sitting on a rickety love seat staring deeply into each other's eyes. As I padded up to the third floor I heard the woman saying urgently, "And I don't want to complicate your life either, but I'm so . . ."

As I rounded the third landing I took out the key to my room, checked the number, and turned left. Then I heard the unmistakable metallic click of the hammer being pulled back on a large-caliber handgun. I saw a shadow in a doorway move and I felt a pipe nudging my skull.

I turned around slowly and saw Emanuel Marco smiling at me from behind a Smith & Wesson .44 magnum. His greasy black hair framed his face, and he smiled like a stray dog with a burr in his mouth.

"Nice gun, Manny, but I think you've been watching too much TV."

"Hey, Cecil, I forgot to mention that I took the guy up on his offer."

I took a step toward him, slowly. "There have been several mistakes made here, Emanuel. First, why would somebody trust you to do a contract murder, because they must know that I'll give you ten thousand dollars to tell me who hired you. You know I can get it from my sister."

I took another small step.

"Nice try, man, but I don't even know who it is. I just talked to the guy on the phone, and picked up half the money in a garbage can. I get half after. Anyway, anyone who pays to have you killed would pay to have *me* killed if I screwed them over. And besides, *he* offered me ten thousand."

Now his back was against the wall. The gun was at my throat.

"Good negotiating. You think they're really going to give you the rest? What are you going to do when they stiff you, go to the Better Business Bureau?"

I took another step forward and now I was too close for him to point the gun at my throat. He had to point it at my chest.

He'd watched enough TV to know that if he fired that cannon off in the hall he would have a hard time sliding out of the hotel on little cat feet. He had one chipped tooth in front, and as he looked at me from behind the gun he poked his tongue through the gap in a nervous twitch. Emanuel had a lot invested in his identity as a small-time criminal, and I knew he was a little nervous about his new role as a killer.

"Back the fuck up, man!" He jabbed me in the chest.

I took one more step forward and I was close enough to smell peppermint schnapps on his breath. The .44 was pointed at my stomach.

"The second mistake, Emanuel, is that you're a fuck-up and wouldn't know how to kill somebody if they were in an iron lung."

I lunged forward and brought my left hand around the barrel and my right down toward the hammer. I stretched the web of my right hand, the flesh between my thumb and index finger, and wedged it under the hammer just as Emanuel pulled the trigger. The hammer snapped down and pierced the skin.

I kneed him in the testicles. There was a long phlegm-choked gasp, and then some gagging.

My hand was bleeding a little and I freed my skin from the gun. I opened the cylinder and ejected all the rounds onto the floor.

He started to move in a crouch toward the stairs and I brought the handle down on the top of his head. One of the walnut grips split off and fell over the edge of the staircase landing.

It's a lot harder to knock a man unconscious than most people think. And it's kind of a spooky thing to nudge a person that close to death or permanent brain damage. But I tapped him twice. His body went limp. I picked up his hand and grabbed him by his hair and dragged him to the door of my room.

I fumbled with my key, pushed the door open, and dragged Emanuel in. Tightly wedged between the plywood wardrobe and the foot of the bed, his head came to rest next to the radiator, which was banging and rattling as if someone in the basement were sending a frantic message.

I tried to fill an ice bucket from the stove-sink-refrigerator unit and got about a cup of rusty water. I threw it on his face anyway. He didn't move but his eyelids fluttered. I squatted above his chest and put my face very near his nose.

"I'm going to listen very carefully to your explanation of who paid you to kill me. Then I'm going to decide whether I need to kill you or not."

"It's the truth, man. I don't know. Hey, I was only going to scare you, you know?"

"Where's the money?"

He pointed to his inside jacket pocket. Then his hand shifted down his leg. I jerked the knife out of his boot. It had an eight-inch black blade. Electrician's tape was wrapped around the tang for a handle. I pressed it against his throat.

His pulse fluttered through his skin at the edge of the blade. I reached in his jacket and pulled out an envelope that held a fat stack of one hundred dollar bills.

"No one gave you this much money to scare me. You have several serious problems, Emanuel, and credibility is not the least of them. Now, who hired you? Think about it. It's important and it has a bearing on your future."

The skin broke under the blade of his knife. A thin line of blood trickled down his neck.

"I swear to God, man, I don't know." His eyes were glazed, his head was shaking slightly, back and forth.

I patted him gently on the shoulder, then I took the knife from his throat and threw it in the sink. Coercion never works in real life like it does on TV.

"I believe you, Emanuel. I really do. But I can't have you following me around."

I put the envelope of money in my back pocket and I swung the butt of the pistol across his forehead. He moaned and lay back.

He kept moaning and his eyes kept fluttering like aspen leaves as I dragged his body parallel to the window and the bed. Now his feet were even with the edge of the radiator. What I wanted to do was set both legs up on the radiator pipe, wedging them firmly between the pipe and the wall. With his torso flat on the floor—head rocking back and forth, moaning—I could stand up on the bed, bounce twice on the mattress, vault forward and land just above his knees. I imagined that they would support me briefly, then snap like pieces of kindling.

But I didn't. Even if Emanuel was a scumbag who was trying to kill me, I kind of liked him. So I stuck his gun in the top of his pants and threw him down the stairs.

EIGHT

WHEN THE POLICE arrived and found him on the second-floor landing, they arrested him on the spot, knowing, of course, that he was a criminal. Their investigation would fill in the details. They'd ask a few questions, and Emanuel might talk, but not about me. He had been half-smart shooting his mouth off in the bar about a contract killing, because it would look improbable, he hoped, that he would be the one to actually do it. But now if he accused me of assaulting him it would look, I hoped, as if he *had* taken the money for the killing.

It wasn't worth worrying about at this point. In the morning I paid my bill in cash and walked up to a French bakery for a croissant and an espresso. I read *The New York Times Book Review*. If I looked at the reviews and maybe the jacket covers I could fake having read the latest trendy books. That kind of thing helped in Juneau but it didn't matter much in Sitka. So I just scanned the poetry section to see if Wendell Berry had anything new and then tried to figure out if the waitress was really speaking French. She finally let me make some phone calls on her private line. Merci.

There is a woman at the phone company business office who does favors for me. Although she doesn't like to see me in the flesh, she is friendly over the phone. Her husband was arrested after he had admitted to his psychologist that he had had sex with the fifteen-year-old daughter of his business partner. I worked on his case and had helped keep him from going to prison by establishing that he was also having sex with the psychologist. They couldn't pay me enough, but they were grateful and would do things to help, as long as we didn't have to be seen together.

When I called her at the office, I gave a false name to the receptionist. Her voice was singsong when she came on the line. "How can I help you, Dr. Face?" But it changed when she recognized my voice.

I gave her a list of names and dates and asked her to find the phone records for me. She agreed and hung up without asking how I'd been since she'd last seen me.

I called another friend out at the airport. I'd met her working on a custody/kidnapping case and we had talked about having an intimate platonic relationship and ended up with an empty-headed sexual one. This time I used my real name. Her voice brightened when she recognized mine. I gave her a list of travel records that I needed and told her that a woman from the phone company would be dropping off an envelope at her office. Most likely, the courier would be wearing a hat, trench coat, and dark glasses but she shouldn't let that worry her.

Then she helped me with my travel plans to Stellar. Nonsmoking. Bulkhead. Aisle. I promised her dinner, a movie, and an uncomplicated evening of sexual intimacy. She said that would be nice as long as her fiancé could pick out the movie. I agreed.

I walked down a winding street past the governor's mansion with its stately columns and totem pole. I needed to get to the bottom of the hill. Instead of walking down the stairs built into the hillside, I took the elevator in the state office building. In the elevator were three men and two women talking politics and carrying cloth briefcases. They were all dressed in expensive clothes: rough wool, brass zippers, and nylon overcoats. There was one guy in coveralls with rubber boots, scabs on his knuckles, and a long smear of grease across his chin. He was carrying papers in his hand and watching the numbers flash by above the door with an expression of panic. It's common to lose ground level in the state office building.

Some old-time Juneau residents like to complain about the Yuppies in town, the hordes of young lawyers and MBAs who have brought the taste of Seattle or San Francisco to this relatively young mining town. There are, of course, the fern bars and the espresso shops and the food carts that sell anything from lox and bagels to halibut enchiladas. It's true, it's not the same town. But it's enough the same; only the food is better and the women are better looking.

Sy's receptionist had a large manila envelope ready for me at her desk. As she handed it over the counter she apologized: Mr. Brown was unable to see me this morning because he had a court appearance. I saw his Burberry on the oak coatrack and I heard his laugh in the back office.

I had a couple of hours to kill before my appointment with Emma Victor. I bought a raisin and cinnamon bagel from a woman standing beside a cart on Franklin Street. She had huge frame glasses like Elvis Costello's and she was learning to play the mandolin. As I licked cream cheese off my fingers I listened to several butchered versions of "A Sailor's Hornpipe" done in swing time.

The sun was out and when I looked straight up at the tallest buildings in town I could see the waterfalls and the yellowing tufts of grass on the bluffs behind them. It was a beautiful morning, and the landscape seemed to press in and make Juneau seem like a smaller, less sophisticated town than it really was.

I was beginning to feel kind of out of sorts about what I had done to Emanuel. So I went over to the law library in the courthouse, sat at a desk in the corner, and copied down the serial numbers of the five grand. Then I took a cab to the hospital and left an envelope with $2,500 and a get-well note in it. He probably deserved half of it for *trying* to kill me, and it left me $2,500 for cab fares.

It was a twenty-two-mile drive out to Tee Harbor, past the mouth of the glacier and around the twisting corners of the coastal road. The driver wasn't excited at first about the prospect of deadheading all the way back until he looked in his schedule and saw there was a ferry in soon at Auke Bay and he might be able to pick up a fare there. An extra twenty gave him some added motivation.

There was a long flight of steps down to the water off the edge of the road. The house was built on pilings over the tidelands. A gangway led to a log dock. A sixty-foot trawler-style cruiser was moored to the dock and beside it was tied a single-engine floatplane. The house had been built of cedar lumber that had grayed with age. It was built back into the hillside with a low profile to the wind. From the water, the house would blend evenly into the forest. The front door was made of two hand-hewn cedar planks. The door knocker was a brass doe's head. When I used it I heard a woman's voice from behind the door call, "It's open!"

Emma Victor was sitting on a round of firewood next to a picture window looking out over the harbor. She had been cleaning a fishing reel and was holding a can of light oil and a clean cotton rag. She wore a blue sweater and her red hair was pulled back in a bun. Her skin was fine white, like old manuscript paper, and her eyes were silty green.

"There're sea lions working some herring out there." She pointed and her hand was steady. I could imagine her holding a fly rod perfectly still.

Out past the point of her deck the sea lions slid through the water in slippery loops, barely disturbing the surface as they appeared, crunching silvery fish in their jaws. An eagle sat on the top of the piling that held the dock in place. It watched the water by the sea lions and ruffled its feathers slightly.

"They've got to eat, might as well be the herring. I don't imagine the herring feel that good about it. But at least they don't dwell on it. Or do you think they do, Mr. Younger?"

"I imagine it's a very short surprise for them."

At her feet was an enormous brown bear rug. The head was mounted with small eyes that seemed like tiny, close-set punctures in the massive skull. There was a plastic tongue curled behind the snarling teeth. The snout was square and as large as a loaf of bread. The taxidermist had wrinkled it slightly to enhance the snarl but he could do nothing about the small lifeless eyes.

"Are you a hunter, Mr. Younger?"

"Not a very good one. But I go out sometimes."

"Uh-huh." And she smiled at me as if I had just failed some important litmus test.

"Well, Louis was a very good hunter. You know, I came from San Francisco. I saw many glamorous things when I was growing up. San Francisco was so beautiful when I was young. Some of the hills were bare and wild like they still are here. The air was sweet and even mysterious. I thought I could never be human in any other place. My family took a trip to Alaska and I met Louis. I fell in love with him, and I spent that first winter with him. My brothers thought that I went off to college, but I came back here. Back then Louis and I did everything together. I don't know if you ever had the experience, Mr. Younger, of a love that just lifts you up off your feet and keeps you there?"

I shook my head but she was staring out to the bay. She turned slightly away from me.

"I remember once we were walking his trap line up north and the weather turned bad. It was dark and he didn't want to take the risk of the long trip back to the cabin. I was cold and tired and I didn't know what I was doing out God knows where. Then he found a hollow where the wind had blown around a stump and we took off our snowshoes and burrowed into the open pocket under the snow. When we crawled in, it was quiet and completely dark. Louis lit a single candle, and oh my. . . ."

She looked back into the room and she worked her hands in front of her eyes slowly as if she were actually touching her vision.

"It was a cathedral, encrusted with diamonds. The snow sparkled so magnificently. The air was still and the wind was very faint out above the snow. I curled into his arms. We made love for the first time in that snow cave, Mr. Younger."

She looked straight toward me, focused on the past but aware of the effect of being blunt.

"We made love, and our breath formed a thick crust on the snow. Then we slept the most beautiful, peaceful sleep. When I woke up I never thought of San Francisco as my home again, and I gave my life to Louis."

She came back from her memory and stared at me across the room.

"Do you think it's healthy to dwell on a death, Mr. Younger?"

"I suppose it depends on whose death and why you have to dwell on it."

"My husband took this bear." She kicked the rug with her toe, hitting the bear on one of its canines. "It was the same year that we were married, out near Mole Harbor on Admiralty Island. Walt Robbins was with him. The bear almost mauled Louis. In fact, it scratched his rifle. Something like that never frightened Louis. He was very young then, and very funny."

There was a picture of Louis Victor above her fireplace. He was standing hip deep in the white water of a northern river, reeling in a king salmon that was dancing with its tail on the surface of the water as if at the photographer's request. Louis's forearms were dark and muscled. He was gritting his teeth.

"It does not surprise me that my mother-in-law would hire you. It does not surprise me and it does not amuse me. What is it that she thinks you can find?"

I sat on the couch facing her and the open stretch of water beyond her window. "She wants me to find the whole truth."

"You're not an Indian, are you, Mr. Younger? Do you understand anything about Indian people?"

"I know enough to know . . . that I know very little. I

know enough to know that a person can't make assumptions."

"Which is more than most people know. But how do you expect to find the whole truth for this old Indian woman when you don't know what the whole truth would feel like to her?"

"I probably will never know what the whole truth feels like. But I'm a curious guy, and I have only one choice and that is to keep going forward and asking questions. When people evade my questions, I know that something is being hidden from me, and I keep pressing. When people seem to tell me everything and nothing appears to be hidden, then I stop looking. For me, that seems to be the truth. But when someone *tries* to stop me, then I have to keep looking."

The eagle slid from the piling into the air as if riding down the face of an invisible wave and plucked a shiny fish from the water. Its wing beats were labored as it flew away with its catch.

"Well, let me ask you a question then, and see if you evade me. What are you charging her?"

"What?"

"I've done some checking on you, Mr. Younger. You come from a good family. Your father was the Judge, wasn't he?"

I nodded.

"He seemed like an honest man. He wouldn't have taught you to exploit an old woman for her money."

"I'm sorry, Mrs. Victor, but any arrangement between me and my client is confidential."

She looked out the window and smiled.

"Professionally said, Mr. Younger. Don't misunderstand me. My mother-in-law was an intelligent woman in her day but now she's old and—you know." She tapped her forefinger against her temple. "She's not as sharp as she once was. And old people often fall victim to the money-making schemes of others. The nurses at the home tell me what goes on with my mother-in-law so that I can protect her. I telephoned you from here the other night as soon as I heard she was thinking of hiring you."

"She called me and asked me to help her. My rates are fair." My stomach sank as I said these last words and I hoped that my teeth were not clenched. "Do you want me not to work on this case for some reason of your own?"

"Listen to me, young man." Her voice was thick, yet hissing. Her eyes seemed darker and closer together. "My husband is dead, and the man who killed him is in prison. What good, besides to your pocketbook, will this investigation do? Our family has been destroyed. Our privacy has been violated time after time and our lives are in ruins. We are the *victims*, for God's sake! That man in prison is sitting in his room just down the road doing . . . doing handicrafts and watching television. He doesn't have a tenth of the sorrows we have. You want to do something useful? Do something to him. Make him feel something close—even close—to what we feel."

She was not crying but was looking at me steadily.

"He should not be alive. He should not be alive to talk or to laugh or to eat good food. He should not have any small pleasures as long as we have to suffer. For years we've suffered, and other women have suffered in the same way. We're being made fools of by the law. The family—the family is the only thing worth dying for and, Mr. Younger . . ." She pointed a steady index finger at my nose. "If it's worth dying for, it's worth killing for."

"You're speaking of Alvin Hawkes's death?"

"Yes, I am. I hope for it every day, but there's no one to punish men for their unspeakable acts against families. You want to do some good for my mother-in-law, for our family? Kill Alvin Hawkes. But don't defile our family."

The sea lions were gone. There was only a slight, ever-widening ripple on the water. I looked at the bear and it stared back with its comical, dead snarl. The clock ticked.

"Could I speak to your children?"

I wanted to close my eyes for the response.

"My children are traveling, Mr. Younger. And *no*, if there is anything that I can do about it, you will not talk to them about anything. I am going to contact my attorney this afternoon."

"Why did you call me and invite me out here if you felt this way?"

"I wanted to see Judge Younger's son for myself and see if I could convince him to give up this foolish investigation."

"Mrs. Victor, I want to ask you about Walt Robbins."

"I imagined that you would have already heard the filthy gossip that has surrounded us since this thing started. Walt Robbins is like many other men who do not respect the sanctity of our family. I'm sure you've heard rumors about the trouble years ago in Stellar. It had nothing to do with the children or with me."

The eagle sat on top of the piling next to the float plane ripping the fish with the point of its beak as it held it in one of its talons.

"Mr. Younger, my children and I are the victims. We do not need our life disturbed any further."

"If I may ask, Mrs. Victor, what are your plans? Are you going to continue the guiding business?"

"You may ask, but then you will have to leave. Neither the

plane nor the boat are of any use to me. I am in the process of trying to sell them both to bring in some income."

"Could you sell them to Robbins?"

"I could sell them to whomever I want, and I don't like your tone. I think it is time that you go."

"What about your son, Lance? Does he want to take over the business?"

"My children's concerns are none of your business. Good-bye, Mr. Younger."

I ambled out of the house. I thought about asking to stay for lunch but I didn't, and I also didn't call for a cab.

I stood on the side of the road next to the stair landing and waited for a car to drive by. I heard a few bird songs in the brush, ravens and perhaps a thrush, the water licking on the rocks below. I imagined a bear snuffling in the shallow roots just out of sight. In half an hour only one car came down the road and it drove past, accompanied by a rush of wind in the Doppler effect that all dangerous-looking hitchhikers know.

Finally, a talkative carpenter stopped his truck and gave me a lift to the Auke Bay store.

Although I hadn't shaved that morning and had a bandage on my hand where a gun had bit me, I didn't feel evil. But the teenage girl behind the glass hot dog carousel scowled at me as she pointed to the pay phone. I needed to call a cab but instead I called my friend at the airport and added two more names to my list. Then I telephoned long distance to the Pioneer Home in Sitka.

After the nurse had been gone for about two minutes, I heard Mrs. Victor's voice on the other end. I introduced myself, because I didn't think she would recognize my voice, but she cut me off halfway through the introduction.

"Your daughter-in-law does not want me looking into this

case. She says I'm exploiting you for your money and that I can't do any good for your family."

"She and I don't see things the same way."

"Mrs. Victor, did your son tell you about any trouble he had in his family life?"

There was a long pause on the line. I could hear shallow breathing.

"My son . . . had done bad things, things I cannot tell you about."

"You hired me to find the whole truth."

Another pause.

"I cannot tell you about these things over the phone. Not standing here at the nursing station."

"I understand. I'm on my way to Stellar. Will I find what I'm looking for up there?"

"I don't know, Mr. Younger. I suppose it depends on how good a hunter you are."

I told her I wanted to see her just as soon as I got back.

Before I hung up, she said, "I will pay you whatever it costs, but I need to know—how much money will it be? I can make arrangements."

"I've decided to do the case for twenty-five hundred dollars, and I've already been paid."

"By whom?"

A little Tlingit kid holding a Dolly Varden trout by the gills was tapping on the phone booth with the edge of a quarter.

"The answer to that is what I hope to find in Stellar."

The kid tapped louder and louder as I called a cab to take me to the airport. A raven stood in the parking lot watching the Dolly Varden swing from his hand.

NINE

THERE ARE SOME questions so graceful that they should
only be asked, because at some point it becomes interrup-
tive to try and answer them.

One of the most time-consuming questions asked in this
part of the country involves where the "real Alaska" is. Most
of the people living north of Haines consider southeastern
Alaska to be a suburb of San Francisco, inhabited by drug-
addled phoneys and bureaucrats, with a few loggers and
fishermen holding on against all odds. The phoneys and the
bureaucrats have an image of the modern white resident of
the north as a 400-pound Oklahoma building contractor
with a 50-pound gold-nugget watchband and an antebellum
attitude toward the darker races. Anchorage falls in the
middle of this mess.

Anchorage grew up too fast to keep pace with its ability to
dress itself. Today its buildings mostly resemble monu-
mental subarctic toasters, all reflective surfaces to steal the
beauty of the surrounding landscape.

Anchorage is hip deep in the twentieth century. In a
downtown bar you can find a deranged redneck watching a

Rams game on the wide-screen TV alongside an arts administrator who is working on a production of *Waiting for
Godot* to tour the arctic villages. Both of them will walk
around the Eskimo man bundled up asleep on the sidewalk,
but the arts administrator will feel an ironic sense of history.

During a heated discussion on the "real Alaska" issue, I
heard a woman from Eagle River say to a man from Tenakee,
"Okay, smart-ass, if Anchorage isn't an Alaskan city, what is
it?" This might be one of those graceful questions. As my
plane was flying over the city in preparation for the landing,
it ran through my mind many times, like the mantra of an
urban planner: "What is it?"

There were several people I would have liked to see but I
wouldn't have time. There was the painter who took a knock
on the head and could then speak Polish; there was one of
the best mandolin players on the West Coast who lived in a
trailer in the spectacular neighborhood of Spenard; and
there was the sewage system engineer who could bench
press 460 pounds. But I only had half an hour between
planes.

On the trip to Anchorage I had read the information from
the airlines file. None of the principals in the case had flown
in or out of Sitka right before or after Todd was shot. Neither
Walt Robbins nor any of the Victors were on the lists. Nor
were there any R. Walters or Victor Lances or the like. I'd
thought of that.

I read through Alvin Hawkes's medical file while I waited
for my Stellar-bound jet to take off. The sun was setting and
the temperature outside was near freezing. I glanced up and
saw the baggage handlers packing cases of beer onto the
conveyor belt. These cases were being checked through as
excess baggage. Stellar is a damp community as far as

alcohol goes. It's illegal to sell liquor but not to possess it. So any trip to Anchorage, whether business or pleasure, requires excess baggage.

If you live in southeastern Alaska and are used to being stared down at by the mountains with your back against the ocean, the country around Anchorage is a reprieve. The horizons are broad and open. The mountains slope up from the tidal flat, cupping Anchorage but not crowding it against the shallow waters of Cook Inlet. There is a much safer feel to landing or taking off in Anchorage than there is in Juneau, where the mountains stick up like granite nets that will catch you if you overrun the runway.

The flight to Stellar takes about an hour by jet. They serve hot pretzels and drinks. Across from me sat a young business couple. The man wore a Harris tweed jacket and gray slacks. The woman wore a tan silk blouse with a scarf and a blue flannel skirt. They both had on leather Top-Siders and maroon parkas. They each ordered white wine and then conversed about some papers the man took out of his leather valise. Behind them, an Eskimo couple sat with their screaming baby. They were both wearing flannel shirts and nylon windbreakers. The man held the screaming child up in front of his grinning face and sang to it. The baby was in flannel pajamas and its hair shone in the light of the reading lamp, frizzing out like the down of a young goose. The father sang softly in Yupik. The stewardess suggested that he give the baby something to suck on, explaining the difference in air pressure on the inner ears could cause pain. She said this once too often and too loud. The father smiled politely and kept singing. The professional couple glanced backward in annoyance and moved their heads closer together to confer.

I had two pretzels and a glass of Jack Daniel's and after I finished reading I stared out the window. We were flying northwest over the mountains toward the delta country of the Kuskokwim. Outside, I could see the snow-covered outline of a mountain peak, and to the north of that peak I could faintly see a flickering light, perhaps a campfire. The temperature on the ground was zero degrees Fahrenheit and the temperature outside the airplane window was minus fifty degrees.

Alvin Hawkes had been a healthy young man. He had been injured once by accident when a tractor slipped off the jacks but had suffered no major illnesses. He did have a problem with motion sickness for which he took medication while working for Victor. There were several notations about this motion sickness because the medication he got, including what he was taking during the last week of Louis's life, had the side effect of blurring his vision and causing a ringing in his ears. Yet elsewhere those symptoms were attributed not to medication but to "anxiety."

I also found that, according to the official measurement, when he entered prison, he was five feet eight and weighed 150 pounds. Louis Victor was six foot three and he'd weighed 212.

It was 8:00 P.M. when we landed in Stellar. It was fourteen degrees, which was cold for this time of year, even in Stellar.

The baggage area was small and sparse. There were ten of us waiting under the tin roof. I wasn't waiting for luggage but to see if I could recognize anyone. A Yupik Eskimo man in an insulated jumpsuit began to throw the luggage off the carts but no one made a move until he started unloading the cases of beer and whiskey. Then people started toward him with purpose.

A man wearing gray wool pants and an old army parka with a wolf ruff came up to me.

"Hello, Cecil."

He smiled and we shook hands ceremoniously. The last time I had seen Edward he had been the translator in a civil case against a bootlegger. The attorney had wanted to find a Yupik word for rapist. There is no precise word, but we came up with an appropriate phrase that satisfied both the court and the witnesses. We lost the case and Edward and I had spent several days in a hunting camp to compensate ourselves for our loss.

Edward looked well. The strength in his body pointed toward the ground. His posture was straight and solid, eyes clear and handshake firm. The rumors were true—he was sober. His handshake, his walk, and even his tone of voice made me think he had been sober for a while. And there was something wary in him. Or at least this was something new that I thought I saw. A barrier. Some mistrust or unwillingness to let down his guard. He knew I wasn't sober, or wouldn't be soon. It was awkward, so instead of spending time on the pleasantries, I went right on.

"Edward, do you know Hannah Elder? She works for the Department of Social Services. She moved here about six months ago."

"She's pretty. You know her?"

"Old friend. Do you know where she lives?"

His eyes were laughing and he scratched his head in a parody of someone who was slow-witted.

"No, I don't think I do."

He laughed and motioned me to carry my bag to the outside. I began to feel a thaw.

"But maybe I can find it. I was supposed to meet my

cousin. He owes me money. He didn't fly in. So I'll take you there."

We stepped outside to get into his truck. Even in the dark you can tell the country is flat, just by the way the wind blows—strong in your ears and in your bones, but without the accompaniment of trees or ocean. It's just a flat bluster that first hits your ears. When coming from Southeastern my instinct is to stand on my tiptoes to get a good look around. At first, the delta looks empty but it holds hidden surprises revealed by just the slightest changes in elevation. Like a sleight-of-hand artist, the tundra distracts you in the distance, then pulls a coin out from behind your ear.

We drove past the jail and the hospital, both large concrete structures with low profiles to the wind. There were street lights in the parking lot that spread lonely circular pools of light onto the snow.

Edward told me about his family, how one girl was a cheerleader for the wrestling team, how the boys were all doing well in school. He told me the hunting seemed to be getting worse and that he didn't know if it was because of the weather or because of his age. He told me all of these things but I had to ask him about them all specifically. He was happy to reply but didn't want to impose his stories on me without an invitation. He invited me to stay with him at his house if he couldn't find where Hannah lived.

We drove out along the edge of the river and finally on one of the high banks we stopped at a small house that stood alone. It had a steeply pitched roof and a window on each side of the door. It looked as if it had been designed from a child's drawing. The light from a window spilled like milk out onto the river.

"I'm pretty sure this is her house. Looks like her stuff."

I offered to pay Edward for gas but he chuckled. It was a tinkling sound and he covered his mouth so it seemed to come from his hand. He stuffed the money back into my jacket pocket while we were both sitting in the front seat of the truck.

"Can I call you if I need a ride?" He shrugged and shook his head as he put the truck in reverse.

I heaved my shoulder against the truck door and stepped out onto the creaking snow. He drove away. The wind sucked up the sound of the motor and he seemed to be gone very quickly. I didn't quite know what I was doing standing in the road getting colder and colder. I hadn't intended to try to see her when I asked Edward about Hannah, but I didn't struggle when he started taking me to her.

No one in the world will tell you that arriving unexpectedly at the door of someone who used to love you is a wise thing to do. No living person would recommend it. Especially when it's fourteen degrees on the lower Kuskokwim.

She came to the door. The light from a small reading lamp inside backlit her shoulder-length blond hair, but the porch light cast an even glow on her face. All of this in the darkness and wind of the delta. An emptiness stirred in my chest as she focused her eyes on me. She wore a purple sweater with a yellow ribbon laced around the neck. I almost laughed to see her still so beautiful.

After a moment she exhaled.

"Oh God . . . what are you doing here?" But she was smiling. I felt that maybe I would still see spring.

"I'm working a case. I needed to come up here."

We walked into her living room. One of Chopin's nocturnes was playing from the speakers of her small tape player. It was the one with the change that she liked so much: the whole notes changing key in the middle of a phrase. The walls had cheap paneling that buckled on the seams. The room smelled vaguely like stove oil and smoked fish. There was a Yupik loon mask hanging above her table, the long neck curving toward the ceiling with carved figures circling it on the ends of slender rods. The figures, small carved fish and the faces of otters, danced in the heat that rose from the oil stove. There was a reproduction of a Morris Graves sea bird hanging opposite it. The table had one chair. There was a futon with a sleeping bag rolled in the corner. A narrow loft looked down on us.

"Two questions. Are you in trouble? And are you still drinking?"

"Someone would like to kill me. In fact, they shot Todd trying, but I don't think that they will follow me up here. And yes, I'm still drinking. But I'm not sure that the two are directly related this time."

She sat in the chair. "Todd? What have you done to Todd?"

She cupped her chin in her hands, rocking back and forth. "What have you done?"

"Listen . . . will you listen, Goddamn it. I'm to blame for a lot of things and I'm willing to accept the responsibility for them if I have to. I'm to blame for the things I said on the night you left. If you want to throw me out for that you'd be right to. But not Todd. . . . You don't know a fucking thing about it, and you're ready to pass judgment. So don't . . . You don't . . . ."

My jaw was set and I couldn't bring myself to look at her, afraid of what might come bubbling up.

I looked out the window. There was snow on the banks of the river, and ice flowed slowly in the broad current. On the plane I had heard that it was raining in Sitka. Sometimes I feel it's been raining since I was a little boy. Tonight the moon was throwing shadows off the smallest tufts of grass that stuck up through the snow. A cloud passed in front of the moon and the shadows lightened.

"You like it here, Han? Better than Southeastern?"

"It's different. It's cold, like another country."

She stood beside me looking out the window.

"Does the cold get into your bones like the rain does? Sometimes I think the rain is like grief that I have to endure."

I looked at my feet. She rubbed her palm between my shoulder blades.

"That's not the rain, Cecil. That's grief. Let's have something to eat."

She cooked two caribou steaks and some boiled cabbage and cheese. I made a salad. She was very excited about a ripe avocado that was bruised and small.

This is a strange country. The world along the river was preparing for the twilight of winter. Somewhere to the north, there were bears digging into burrows on hillsides, rolling in the smells of caribou and moose grease. There were ptarmigan squatting behind small hummocks out of the wind, whales drifting above the shoals of great underwater canyons. But nowhere would there be anything as peculiar as this little weary avocado, which had probably been raised in sandy soil near the Mexican border, then picked, packed, trucked, barged, flown, trucked again, displayed, purchased, brought home and peeled to be put in our salad, which we would eat with a mouthful of caribou steak.

Hannah drank water and I had iced tea. I saw long-necked bottles of beer in the refrigerator but none were offered.

"You've got another case. You're making money? You seem to be successful now. But the thing I can't understand, Cecil—" She took a bite of her steak. She had a particular way of holding her fork in her fist like a gavel. She pointed it at me. "Everybody knows that all the rules agreed to by groups of men favor the most aggressive and most talented men. So how can you succeed? You're neither aggressive nor talented."

"But"—and here I sipped my iced tea to match her theatrical pauses—"I'm great in bed and have no fear of death."

"Is that why it was Todd who got shot?"

Playfulness would not help me. "Todd got shot because someone is trying to keep me from looking into Louis Victor's death."

"Louis Victor? I thought that was settled long ago."

"Apparently not."

I cleared the table. I had been sitting on a crate and I moved it back to the corner. Then I started doing the dishes. I filled her in on everything I knew about Louis Victor and Alvin Hawkes and Todd's shooting. I left out the part about Emanuel being in the hotel because I didn't want her to change her opinion of my aggressiveness.

Hannah dried. I finished washing and began to wipe the counters and the stove top. The aluminum grease traps under the burners were thick with scum. I took off the grates and washed them. I had to ask for a steel wool pad.

"So what's in Stellar?" she asked.

She reached up high in the cupboard and put away the

salad bowl. I saw the rounded curve of her stomach as her sweater lifted up.

"The Victor family used to live here, and I heard that they had some problems back then. I want to find out about them. Maybe you can help. I might need some Social Service records."

"Cecil, if the problems you're talking about involve domestic violence or sexual assault you know I won't help you. Those are protected documents."

"Okay, I know, but could you at least look at them? Just read them yourself. If there's something there, something that might help, will you tell me?"

She started slowly shaking her head as if the desire to do so was welling up from her feet.

"You want to know if there's a history of abuse or sexual assault in the family? You want me to reveal all the nasty details?"

"Hannah, I'm holding myself back from saying 'It's a nasty business.'"

"Good!"

She grabbed one of the grease traps out of my hand.

"I'll read the reports but I won't tell you anything that was said in confidence. Cecil . . . I can't. I know you have a commitment to the pursuit of your own flaky version of the truth. . . ."

". . . And to finding out who shot Toddy and to saving my own ass. . . ."

"Right . . . and that's what you have to do. But I have equally strong feelings about my commitment. It's something I take seriously. What do you take seriously?"

"Is this going to be a sermon? Do I get a pamphlet along with it?"

"No, it's not."

She looked at me with an expression devoid of playfulness or respect.

"I feel like I compromised a lot during my life with you. I compromised my whole notion of what courage and commitment should be. I'm not going to get sucked into your shifting standards of what justice is anymore. I'm not going to compromise anything anymore just for the sake of this visit."

"Is it too much of a compromise if you read the files on the Victors and Robbinses, and tell me if there is anything there, anything that could enlighten me on why someone wants me whacked?"

"I told you what I'd do. And I'll do that for Toddy, and to get you out of Stellar."

Her hands were shaking slightly. She grabbed another grease trap from my hand.

"You know, I never asked you to wash these . . . damn . . . things."

She pulled the plug in my soapy water. Her fingers were slippery and warm. I dried my hands on a dish towel that was looped through the handle of the refrigerator, then I unzipped my bag and took out the folder I had picked up from Sy Brown's receptionist.

"I'm not trying to rub your nose in it, Hannah, but look at these photographs. It's an eighteen-year-old girl who was supposed to be a witness in the Hawkes trial."

I took out the photographs and stood next to her by the sink.

"It's De De Robbins. The police in Bellingham say she drowned herself because she was pregnant with the child of a married boyfriend. And maybe that's pretty upsetting in Bellingham. But look closely at the photos."

Hannah looked carefully at the pictures, and as I spoke she looked at my face. Her eyebrows were arched in a sad question. Her eyes focused as if she were looking into a deep pool.

I showed her the autopsy shots and some of the police photos. De De lying on the planking of the dock, her arm and shoulder bent back and underneath her torso in a manner no living person could tolerate. Her pants unbuttoned. Her shirt torn. Hannah flipped past those and looked at the autopsy photos. She took deep breaths.

"What's the matter with her arms and her chest?"

"She tried to climb out of the water. She grabbed on to a piling that was covered with barnacles and mussels. She must have struggled to get out. I've seen that before with drunks who fall off a dock."

Hannah frowned.

"But look at this one. Look carefully at the wound on top of her forehead."

"She could have banged her head struggling, couldn't she?"

I held the photograph to the light and we put our heads together. "Look at the curve of the wound and look at the little dots in the middle, set back from the edge. That's a heel mark."

"You're very clinical about this." She looked up at me with disgust.

"You *have* been away a long time. What use is my grief to her now?"

"She left a suicide note?"

"She left a note that said she was scared and depressed. She said she wanted to die. Depressed people get murdered sometimes, too."

"Why didn't the police pick up on this—the head wound and all? I mean, Cecil, you're not exactly a criminology genius."

"I guess the obvious thing to say is they aren't either. But, Hannah, you know cops. They're busy. They've got fights to break up and accidents to go to. They never wanted this to be a murder. And a head wound is not that uncommon in a drowning. It's just a little thing that, added to the others, makes it look . . . weird. Cops don't have much time for weird."

"It seems that you have plenty. Who would want her dead? Who was there?"

"I don't know. I don't . . . know."

"So where does your not knowing lead you? Are you making any progress or not?"

"God, you're snotty. I don't think that she killed herself, okay? I think someone didn't want her to testify. I think Alvin Hawkes was meant to go down hard and someone was afraid that the self-defense claim might fly, and wanted to insure that it wouldn't. Hannah, I think that the same person killed Louis Victor, and then De De Robbins. A person is walking around someplace who has nothing to lose by killing again."

She took the pictures and held them with her dish towel as if the photographs themselves were bloody.

"She was eighteen?"

I nodded and took the photo from her. I sat down on the edge of the futon and considered what I wanted to say. Suicide, murder. It can be impulsive: an unformed thought that suddenly becomes an action, the surprise ending in the story you tell about your life. The story you constantly repeat to yourself and revise. Then, in one version, you follow a thread that leads to the impulsive death of someone else or, maybe, yourself. The narrative of your life doesn't take you there but the context of the story does.

I was collecting jumbled facts but I couldn't put them together to tell a story. I stood up and walked back toward the sink.

"She'd been a deckhand on her father's boat. She was the only one to see some kind of struggle on the beach. The day before she would have testified, she was killed. Hawkes was in jail and he wouldn't have wanted her dead if her testimony would have helped him. Hawkes could have killed Louis Victor but he would have had to overcome the fact that he was about sixty pounds lighter than a man who was a professional hunter, armed, and in excellent shape. And he would have had to get off a lucky shot to have hit Louis in the head because the medication he was taking blurred his vision."

"But you said yourself Hawkes doesn't deny that he killed Louis. How are you going to get around that in court?"

"My client isn't concerned with the courts. This is a personal problem. If Hawkes didn't do it, what happened? There were four other people in the bay that night—De De Robbins; her father, Walt; Norma Victor and Lance Victor. So I need you to look at those records for me. I need to know if there is anything that can tell me why any of them would want to kill Louis."

"I told you. I'll look tomorrow."

She walked away from the sink and sat down near the stove with her head leaning against the wall. A strand of her hair fell forward and curled against her throat. It bobbed in time with her steady pulse. She knew I was going to spend the night. She wasn't going to throw me out and she wasn't going to call Edward to haul me away, like garbage. I could sleep on the floor near the oil stove, and as she slept in the loft she would smell my presence like the wet coffee grounds and avocado skin in the compost bucket. And in the morning I would be there to be dealt with. I watched her run these thoughts through her mind. Her face was half lit by the thin light from the reading lamp. I imagined the skin on her left cheek to be warm.

I put the pictures of De De Robbins back in my bag.

There are questions that should not be answered but I never know which questions those are.

TEN

THERE ARE SOME tricks to hunting by industry. Deception can play a part.

The courthouse in Stellar is a small brown building set on pilings above the tundra. There is a meeting room, a business office, a courtroom, and the office of the court clerk. It's here that the public records are kept.

That morning the courtroom was filled with the voices of several people arguing at once. In one corner of the outer lobby a young white woman in blue jeans and a flannel shirt was speaking softly in English to an Eskimo man. She was explaining the difference between nolo contendere and guilt. He had a swollen eye and bruised knuckles. He nodded his head and looked at his hands.

I asked to see the card catalog for the case files. The woman beamed up at me. The lines of her face limned various circles, her eyes sparkled. Before she could answer me her telephone rang. I waited patiently, leaning against the wall, until she was free.

"They are all on our new computer," she told me. "Do you have a name and a case number?"

I gave her Louis Victor's name. She quickly typed in the information and waited. There was nothing. She frowned and tapped the space bar. Then she waited, staring into the monitor. Waiting.

"There should be something. Even if we don't have the name we should get something."

Two of her friends came over and I helped them tap the space bar, wiggle cords, and see if things were plugged in securely. The screen stayed dark. Finally, she said, "Well, we can let you into the file room and you can see what you can find. It's really not that big. Nita will show you in."

Nita led the way to a door that was locked. After much fumbling with the keys, we stepped into the file room; 20-by-30 floor to ceiling, four rows of court records encompassing more than fifteen years. Nita showed me where the coffee pot was and I started in on the files. She went back to her office.

I would fix their computer on the way out, if they hadn't already figured it out by then. At first I had just unplugged it from the wall, then I had unplugged the monitor, and then I had unplugged the computer end of the main power cord. We had all been helpful, tapping and checking the cords. All I had had to do was keep checking cords and making sure one was a little loose while the ladies made sure the others were tight. It was a lot better for me to be alone in the file room. I could almost founder in a room so full of information.

I found a file for Walt Robbins. All it showed was one appearance for driving while intoxicated. I slipped his file back into the stacks.

I found the 1966 case file on Louis Victor. The grand jury had considered a charge for assault in the second degree.

There were pages of notes and motions; there was a manila envelope with a red seal that was stamped "Confidential—Not for Public Record."

I stepped behind the stacks and carefully began to peel the tape back.

The door opened and Nita stuck her head in. "You finding what you need?"

"Yes, thank you," I answered, a cheerful note in my voice.

"Oh, good," she said, and I heard her footsteps coming closer. I pressed the tape down firmly with my thumb and began reading one of the pages of a motion.

"We got the computer up again. Maybe I can help."

"Oh, no thanks." I waved the file gaily. It was beginning to feel warm in my hand.

"Oh, good," she said, then added, "I just better make sure that there isn't any confidential material in there."

Busted.

She took the manila folder out of the file and handed me back the useless legal documents. "There ya go!"

So much for cleverness; on to pure industry. For the next three hours I came up with common Eskimo, Armenian, Filipino, and Caucasian names and had Nita running back and forth to the file room. Every time I saw her pour a cup of coffee I asked her for a new string of names. With each file her professional cheeriness began to lessen. It was twelve o'clock exactly when I asked her for a series of case numbers including Louis Victor's. Other people in the office were putting on their coats and were waiting for her.

She set the pile of files on her desk. "You're going to have to hurry because it's lunchtime and we close for an hour."

She went through the files, taking out the confidential envelopes. I glanced at them briefly one by one. Nita shifted from one foot to another. I could tell her feet were beginning to hurt. I handed her back the files. She put the envelopes back in and started toward the file room.

"Oh my gosh, Nita, I forgot!"

"What?!"

"I have to make a copy of one of the original complaints for my boss."

"I'm sorry, but I'm going to lunch." She turned and started to walk away.

"It won't take a second."

I walked up to her and took the Victor case file from the pile in her arms and started walking toward the copying machine in the back office. Luckily, I could work with my back to the people waiting for lunch. I opened the file and slipped my thumb under the red seal. I took out all of the papers and copied everything on the six sheets of paper, resealed the envelope the best I could, and caught Nita as she was coming back out of the file room.

"Thank you. You were very helpful."

"The next time you should try to be more organized." She was putting her coat on as she scolded me.

"I know." I thanked her again and walked out.

I walked the half mile to the only hotel and restaurant in town, the Delt Inn. The sign above the door showed a hand of playing cards fanned out in a full house. The sun was out, although lower on the horizon than I was used to in the fall. The sunlight was a milky pastel and the shadows were blurred and mixed with the darkness. The snow was not deep but already people were driving snowmachines along the right-of-way. Several of the buildings I passed were Quonset huts, others were frame houses with thin plywood sheeting, old oil stoves pumping like steam engines on the inside. There were countless sled dogs. I couldn't see any trees or fire plugs, but lots of dogs. When one, tied in the yard of a cabin, started barking, dogs from a great distance would answer and soon it sounded like a pounding surf of dog voices.

Standing by the side of the road, I opened the file that I had copied. Two pages contained a psychological evaluation of Emma and Louis Victor's daughter, Norma. The other pages were notes taken by a court reporter that were meant to accompany a child's taped statement. I leaned up against an oil drum that was inexplicably sitting next to the road. I read through the profile of the nine-year-old Norma Victor.

In the opinion of the examiner, Norma was a deeply confused child, with "fundamental questions about identity." She was "experiencing sexual awareness but had no reference point by which to incorporate it into her problem-solving capabilities." Toward the end of the report the last paragraph led off with:

Concerning the suspected sexual abuse, the child N. V. does not acknowledge any such activity. She describes a loving, almost reverential attitude toward L. V., her father, and the suspected perpetrator. Yet because of her anxiety in the areas related to sexuality and because of her periods of depression and hostility, it is recommended that the family enter into a voluntary program to monitor its members' interaction.

On the front of the report there was a box for the name and date of first agency contact. Beside the date was the name Emma Victor.

As I walked toward the inn I began to notice more and

more empty plastic liter bottles of Canadian whiskey. Often they'd be sunk in the snow surrounded by the stains of the last swigs of the contents, like strange animal scat. On the porch of the hotel, men were standing around talking, smoking, with those plastic bottles down the fronts of their jackets. Occasionally, they would step behind the side of the building and share a drink.

There's an arctic entryway at the inn. As I walked into the dimly lit lobby I saw several people sitting on the floor. There was one very old couple. The woman was wearing a beautiful muskrat parka pieced together with marten trim and a wolf ruff. She was sitting with her legs flat on the floor, stretching straight out in front of her. Her mukluks pointed toward the ceiling. She was holding hands with her husband. She was speaking with Edward.

He gave me a short bow from the waist. "This is my grandmother's sister and her husband from Hooper Bay. They've come down to go to the hospital."

We shook hands all around, with smiling and nodding.

"Everything all right with them?"

He shrugged. "The public health nurse told them to come. They don't know that they're sick. They came anyway." He gestured around the room to include everyone in the entryway. There was a girl slumped in the corner. She was wearing only a white T-shirt, blue jeans, and her pack boots. She was breathing. I checked.

I offered to buy Edward lunch. As he made explanations to his family, I went inside and got us a booth.

There was a TV on a stand hanging from the ceiling above the stainless steel pie case. On the screen a man in a black leather suit was swinging an electric guitar as if it were an ax laying into a plate-glass window.

Edward slipped into the booth opposite me. He looked up at the TV and grinned. His teeth were very white but several of them were missing.

"I don't like TV so much." Again he smiled. "Too many white people."

"Don't you like any TV?"

"I like Los Angeles's Magic Johnson." He looped his arm over his head in the imitation of a hook.

We ordered hamburgers and drank coffee while we waited.

"Did you know Louis Victor?"

"He was a pretty good hunter. He had a Yupik girlfriend. He was Indian, I think. His girlfriend's brothers are pretty good, too."

"He had a girlfriend here while he was married?"

"People knew about it. He would hunt with her and drink with her. She was real pretty. I heard that he really liked her."

"What about his wife?"

"I don't know, maybe she didn't like Eskimos or Indians either one. I saw her once with a broken nose. Maybe he hit her but I don't know."

"What about the other woman?"

"She lived upriver with her family. I heard that Louis's wife was gonna kill her. I don't know, I hear lotsa things."

"What else did you hear?"

"Louis's wife went south, I guess to be with her family. Some of her brothers came back here. They got drunk one night and said they were going to kill Louis. Said that it was dangerous for their sister to sleep with a man if he was . . . violent."

Edward smiled as he recounted this last. An enigmatic

grin, which seemed a mixture of pity and suppressed anger. He wiped his mouth and then put on a more polite smile.

"The brothers were from San Francisco. They were big shots in the police department—Cecil, do you think that I'm stupid?"

"Christ, where'd that come from?"

Our hamburgers arrived, ground beef on buns that came out of ovens two thousand miles away, wilted lettuce, and weary tomato slices. Edward looked down at his sadly as if it were a sign of his own failure.

"Some people make me feel stupid. They don't know anything; they ask *me* for things . . . for information. But even when I have to translate so they can understand, they make me feel stupid. Emma Victor's brothers were that kind. Big white men who stand up straight all the time with their arms folded."

I was chewing on the rubber meat. I thought about Louis Victor sneaking away to his Eskimo lover and beating his white wife. I realized he would have started to beat his lover given time. On a particularly evil drunken night, just before Hannah left, she accused all men of being motivated by death. I didn't understand it then and I'm not sure I understood it any better now.

"What do you know about Eskimos, Cecil?"

"I don't know shit about Eskimos."

"You feel stupid?"

"Sometimes."

"Your father, did he make people feel stupid?"

"I think he did, but he wouldn't admit it. I think he'd call it something else, not stupid."

"What would he call it?"

"Their failing."

He smiled at me again. "Your father, the Judge, was he really smart?"

"Shit, Edward, what is this? I guess he was smart. Maybe he talked more than you but he wasn't any smarter."

We sat in silence and ate until the hamburgers were gone. Then we were done eating and were sipping coffee for a moment.

"You know, Cecil"—he leaned forward—"lots of people say you're an asshole, but I think you're pretty good."

I dabbed the stub of a french fry in the residue of my ketchup. I traced a five-pointed star, then several circles. I'm not so good with compliments.

Hannah walked into the restaurant. There was the sound of hissing grease and the smell of cigarette smoke in the air, the clatter of dishes and the consonant thrumming of Yupik being spoken. She stood framed in the doorway: She had her parka draped over her arm and she wore clean blue jeans, a burgundy blouse, and a silver pendant of a killer whale around her throat. On her feet she wore white snow boots, with the laces undone. She stood in the doorway surveying the crowd as if this were the Oak Room at the Plaza Hotel. Edward and I weren't hard to see but she stood there for several seconds looking. Everyone, even people with great confidence, should be allowed some vanity. Finally, without any nod of recognition, she started to walk toward our table.

Edward had not seen her; he was looking down at my plate. He leaned forward and whispered, "You need to learn the story about the bears."

Before I had time to ask him another question, Hannah sat down next to Edward. With a rustle of nylon she slid her parka behind her back.

"Christ, Cecil, I don't know why I get into these things

with you anymore. I almost got into a real situation looking up those files."

"You going to say hello to Edward?"

She stopped. "I'm sorry. We've met before, haven't we?"

Edward smiled and raised his eyebrows to indicate yes.

Hannah smiled back at him and then turned a frown on me. "I didn't mean to be rude but Mr. Younger's got me going. I never liked his kind of work and now he's got me doing it."

Edward gave her a full smile: curves and echoes of curves, and then he picked up the gloves and hat that he had wedged down into the seat of the booth.

"I gotta go. Maybe we'll talk about it later. Okay?" Hannah stood up and let him out. I waved at Edward with a french fry.

"Did I interrupt something?" she asked.

"That's okay. What did you find out?" I continued my ketchup painting.

"Well, there was an investigation concerning Louis Victor. There are no substantiated charges. I'm not going to tell you any more."

"Come on, Hannah. You know how serious this is. You already looked it up. You already broke the rules. So tell me."

She sighed. "Apparently, he beat his wife, and a teacher suspected there was some sexual abuse going on. Emma and Lance gave statements but nothing was ever confirmed. And Norma testified at a Child in Need of Aid hearing. She said that there'd been no abuse. She broke down and pleaded that she loved her dad. But that behavior is consistent with a child who has been abused."

"It's also consistent with a girl who loved her dad."

"Don't start, Cecil."

"Did they break up the family?"

"He was ordered to stay away from them during the criminal investigation and the legal proceedings, then he was ordered by the judge to go get alcohol counseling."

"Did he live with his girlfriend during that time?"

"I don't know. In the reports it just said he was staying with friends. I suppose you've seen the court records?"

I nodded, and licked a spot of ketchup off my finger.

"Is there any evidence that he sexually abused his daughter?"

"No. All we have is a confused girl who is devoted to her mom and dad. She was caught in the middle of a war between the two. Not an extraordinary story."

I thought for a moment and then asked, "What about Walt Robbins?"

"There is nothing in our records about him. That is, other than the fact that his old address was listed, by the mother, Emma Victor, as a possible home for placement of her two kids. Although he wasn't married at the time, his house was considered a safe house."

"What about De De?"

"De De was his, from a marriage that had broken up years earlier."

"What happened to his wife?"

"I heard she died."

"You know how she died?"

"Cecil, give it up. Louis Victor is dead. They have a killer in jail. They aren't going to let Hawkes out of jail and open up an investigation into the possible motives of Walt Robbins. You know they aren't."

"Nobody arrested the person who killed De De Robbins. The person who killed her didn't want Hawkes to get off."

"You think Robbins waited for years to get Louis? That he then killed his own daughter because she was going to blow his alibi? Doesn't it matter that Alvin Hawkes, insane as he seems to be, virtually admits he killed Louis?"

"He also says that there are voices being transmitted from the center of the earth. And if Hawkes is the mastermind behind this, who shot Toddy? Who is trying to kill me?"

The plates were cleared away, and now I had nothing to dabble with, but I twisted a napkin into a tight knot.

"Maybe it's unrelated. Any number of the wacky friends you end up drinking with are capable of taking a shot at you. These events are more likely random than not. Face it, Cecil, you don't have a theory."

"I don't know. Maybe Lance and Norma . . ."

"The kids? Weak, Cecil. Did they shoot Toddy, too?"

"I dunno. . . ." The napkin was a knotted coil between my fingers.

"The kids are here in Stellar. And they have been for about two weeks."

"Both of them?"

"Both Lance and Norma. On the night that Toddy was shot, they were here. Nowhere near Sitka."

I set the white greasy snake of the napkin down carefully, almost formally, on the fat-streaked table. On the TV a montage of images from the news was flashing across the screen in time to thumping synthesized music. A general with arms upraised, a soldier and a dark-skinned baby. The crowd had thinned out in the restaurant but there was still plenty of noise.

A man walked by outside with five sled dogs tethered together. I could see they were all yipping and pulling in different directions. The man, in snow boots and traditional parka, was straining against them and moving his mouth but I couldn't hear the dogs or his voice.

"I want to talk to them. I want to talk to the kids."

"I think Lance and Norma are staying in one of those shipping-box houses down by the river."

"Can you take me there?" I asked as I stood up and put on my coat.

We walked outside through the arctic entryway filled with men and women talking and dozing off. We came out into the full cacophony of sound: the dogs barking, the man yelling, the snow machines along the highway chattering along like chainsaws on skis. I felt drowsy myself and would rather have stayed in the doorway drinking Canadian whiskey from a plastic bottle.

Hannah watched me hesitate. She had her parka on and a scarf across her face. She touched my arm.

"You're such a baby when your theories don't pan out."

Right then I didn't care to be in Stellar, talking to a woman who used to love me.

I put my arm around a man in the corner. "Give me a drink, okay?" He did. I offered him a buck but he smiled and wouldn't take it. I took one long swallow, wiped my mouth, and walked toward Hannah's truck.

ELEVEN

HANNAH DROPPED ME down by the slough, pointed her finger toward a stack of empty cargo containers, and drove away, the thin crust of snow squeaking slightly under her tires.

I guess it doesn't bother me that most of the time I live in an imaginative world the size of an overturned teacup. But in the minutes that I walked away from Hannah's truck down the banks of the lower Kuskokwim, my dream was as broad as the actual horizon. I had the illusion of seeing everything. The mountains were as distant as abstract thought, the river was intimate and real. I took two deep breaths and felt my eyes widen. My feet sank only slightly in the hard sandy soil. I walked upstream.

It was cold by the river. I wasn't dressed for anything but chatting in a café. I shifted from foot to foot, trying not to look conspicuous in my leather coat and thin-soled shoes. Two dogs barked at me from the ends of their chains. Shipping pallets were stacked in piles. I was so out of place, I could have fallen to the tundra from the enormous sky.

My chest felt empty. I was cooling off quickly. A small boy

walked by in a parka, blue jeans, and insulated boots. I asked the kid if the Victors were around. He didn't look up at me, but pointed at the stack of cargo containers and wiggled his boot toe in a chunk of dirt that was free of snow where a fuel can had sat overnight. He pointed again, as if he were telling on somebody.

I walked upstream around two bends of the river that were fortified by pilings. Flat-bottomed fishing skiffs, drift boats with their outboard engines propped up, were hauled up on the hardened mud of the riverbank. The river was slow and brown, tired at the end of the season and speaking softly. The air was cold but still damp with the fall.

I slipped several times making my way over the rough-hewn levee, then I popped down on the other side into what looked like somebody's camp. There were four freezer vans, the kind hauled by truck and then loaded by rail to be shipped by barge. The mail boat. The bringers of avocados and even snow machine parts. These containers are the fifty-gallon drums of the post-oil boom. They were blocked up on pilings and between them was a pitched shed roof. The whole arrangement made a kind of open-air compound. You could live inside the vans and work out under the roof. There was a wood fire in an upright steel drum sitting at the back edge of the roof line. Dried fish hung in strings, their bodies split open and dangling loosely like strange tropical leaves. There was a radio playing from somewhere in the darkness of one of the containers. On the right side of the vans there was a snow machine with the cowling off and parts of the engine spread out on top of a carpet of cardboard. The smell was a faint mixture of oil, disinfectant, dried fish, and sewage.

I saw an old Sunbeam percolator sitting on top of an outboard engine mounted on a rack: plugged in, light on, nothing bubbling in the half-moon glass top. I reached for the mug on top of a footlocker and heard the sickeningly familiar sound of a shell being jacked into a chamber.

"I don't think I know you." A woman's soft voice reached up and buzzed like a bug in my ear.

I turned around. I was too self-conscious to raise my hands in the air, and was feeling too stupid to be either smart-assed or belligerent.

"I'm sorry. My name is Cecil Wayne Younger."

I spoke into the dark opening of the container. I thought if I gave my whole name it would have more of a ring of truth. I had walked smack into someone's home without realizing it and now I stood a good chance of being shot. I winced, and tried to look goofy and nonthreatening.

"What kind of name is Cecil Wayne Younger?" At least this was a good question, and the beginning of a discussion.

"It's Scottish—at least, I think it's Scottish. Listen, I was wondering, if you are planning to shoot me, do you think we could talk a little first?"

"I'm not going to shoot you, Cecil Wayne Younger. I was just wondering why someone dressed like a Juneau pimp was wandering around helping himself to my coffee."

She stepped into the light and cranked the shell out of a small-caliber rifle. She was a young woman, with high cheekbones and a narrow nose. She held her thumb down into the magazine to keep the next shell from advancing. She closed the breech, leaned the rifle against the side of the door, and jumped down onto the dirt. She was wearing brown insulated coveralls over a purple hooded sweatshirt.

She had short black hair, tied back with a red bandanna. Her voice was rough, almost raspy, but with a child's cadence, as if she had memorized everything she was saying.

"You *are* from Juneau, aren't you?"

"How'd you know?" I asked, afraid of the answer as soon as I had spoken. The most identifiable Juneau pimps worked in the legislature and it hurt me to be confused with them. Especially here on the lower Kuskokwim.

"We've lived down there. I think I might have seen you before."

She looked at me with a steady brown-eyed gaze and as I returned the stare she broke off eye contact and started looking for a cup. She didn't have the assurance of her grandmother.

As I watched her look for a cup that was right in front of her she brushed away hair that had long ago been cut off. She curled the tips of her fingers up and around her ears, scooping at hair that wasn't there. She did this three times, and when she saw I was watching she curved her palm around her head to make it seem like she was scratching her neck.

"Your name is Norma, isn't it?"

She looked back up at me with a sudden start, like a doe caught in the headlights.

"You're that detective guy. . . ."

The cup fell off the footlocker into a pile of box-end wrenches. I reached down and picked it up. The porcelain was chipped and there was grease on the handle. I squatted by the pile of tools and handed it up to her. She had to walk closer to me to reach it. She didn't want to. I was left with the cup.

She curled the long hair of her childhood over the stubble

above her ears. She looked straight at the ground and not at
me or the cup. Smoke passed in front of the opening of her
hood, though I'm sure she didn't notice. The wind blustered
in and the fish swung on their strings, knocking the hard-
dried flesh together slightly.

"You're that detective guy Momma talked about. You're
after Gram's money. She's a crazy old lady and Mom says
you're going to run up all kinds of bills and charge her a
million bucks to open up the old stuff, the old . . . stories."

"I guess there are some stories that are older than others.
A friend of mine was shot the other day."

A man spoke from the darkness. "She's a hard life, isn't
she?"

The new voice was deep but still somewhat nasal. Around
the corner came a young man dressed exactly like Norma
Victor but with a torque wrench in his hand. His voice and
his muscles were tight. He had a rolling sway to his walk. His
chin was cocked up, and his head swayed slightly as if he
had bad eyesight and was scanning the area to locate me
more accurately by smell.

"She's a hard fucking life for a guy with nothing better to
do than dig up garbage."

"I take it we're talking about me," I said, with a happy
songbird note in my voice.

The end of the torque wrench appeared a quarter of an
inch in front of my nose. It appeared so suddenly I didn't
have time to be startled. I was more fascinated. It was almost
like a parlor trick.

"You're absolutely correct . . . we're talking about you."
His voice smoldered like the deepest layers of wet compost.
His breath was in my face. The wrench did not waver.

"Well, I just wanted to be clear."

Startled women with high-powered rifles are something to be wary of, but angry men with torque wrenches—if they can't be teased into a good mood—are more dangerous, at least in the short term.

He gave me just the slightest bump on the bridge of the nose. Painful, but almost friendly in its restraint. The pain fanned out up my forehead like a bad memory from childhood. His arrogance was so thick he was *pleased* to be insulted by an underling. I stopped smiling.

The wrench hung in the middle ground between us. His eyes were black and his hair almost scalp-shiny short. He was obviously Norma's brother, Lance, and he was not smiling either.

"You're right. I was stupid blundering in here, and I'm sorry. I am. All I want to do is have a short talk about your grandma and why she would want me to look into an old case that no one else wants examined. That's all I want to do. . . ."

His eyes brightened, and the roll of muscle around the hump of his shoulders relaxed. He came off the balls of his feet.

"And if you hit me again with that wrench, I'm going to try and kick your lungs out."

He smiled, and reached down for the coffee cup that was still dangling from my finger. He knew a bluff when he heard one. He poured himself some coffee from the Sunbeam. He walked back under the edge of the roofline and looked out over the river and the tundra to the north. He had his back to me, and puffs of vapor came over his shoulder as he spoke.

"Nothing. Nothing at all."

Pieces of cut-up pallets burned and popped in the fire at the bottom of the drum. A black bird walked the soft mud

flat by the river, and beyond the river the tundra was hiding
itself in low rises that shortened the horizon and brought
distance closer in.

"You know what I see when I look out there?"

The fire sizzled and I held my tongue. I'm a sucker for
stepping on rhetorical questions but this was not the time.
He slumped forward a little and shoved the toe of his boot
into the top of a motor oil carton that happened to be lying in
front of him.

"I see nothing. Nothing to get in my way, and nothing to
stop me from doing exactly what the fuck I want to do. That's
what wilderness is for. That's what brought the pioneers
here. I like it. It makes me feel good. You know I could feed
you to this river and nobody would give a shit."

"It's a great country, isn't it?"

Norma moved in between us, looking down as if she had
misplaced something and was just happening to look for it.

"Lance . . . come on. We don't need to . . . do anything."

She looked up at her older brother. I could see her eyes;
they were pleading. There is scant shelter from violence in
this country and it didn't look like this lean-to would do for
her any longer.

"Let him go."

Fuck it. This was getting like a ping-pong game.

"The trouble is, Norma, I'm not going anywhere, so
maybe he *is* going to have to . . . do something."

Thinking back on it, I can't believe I said this. As much
as I worry about getting into confrontations, when I find
myself in the middle of one I get a little giddy. Or maybe
stupid.

The muscles in Lance's back bunched; he looked almost
as if he had a hump and his eyes were narrowing.

"Calm down, pal. All I want to know is why would your grandma want to hire me after all this time? It's all wrapped up. Why doesn't she think so?"

"My grandma is an old, crazy Indian. She doesn't trust anything that white courts or police do. She . . ."

"She doesn't accept his death," Norma said as she moved behind me and poured herself some coffee. She brushed back her imaginary hair. Her eyes darted between Lance and the ground as she spoke.

"She can't accept the fact that she bears some responsibility for his death."

"What's her responsibility?"

"Alvin Hawkes was . . . is . . . some kind of cousin. He's related to our grandfather's people in Illinois. Grandma asked Dad to hire Hawkes for the season. His family thought that coming to Alaska would do him some good. She was the one who brought him out here. She set it up so it could happen."

Anvils. I looked out at the tundra. Was this whole thing just about the old lady's guilt? If she hadn't helped arrange the job for Hawkes, would her son still be alive? If I just showed her that she wasn't to blame, would that be the whole truth?

The little boy with the parka was rolling a bicycle wheel without a tire in the mud. It left two narrow parallel tracks. He could roll that wheel a thousand miles upriver and the tracks would never meet. But anvils do not fall out of the sky.

"Look, I bet you have a morbid curiosity. You want to see something?" Lance asked.

He walked over to the container door where his sister stood. He reached up into the shadow and brought down a rifle.

Norma winced and turned her back on him. "Lance, don't!"

"Come on, take a look. This is a 45-70. It's the one that killed my dad. It took some doing but I got it back from the police. I had to rebuild the stock and some of the parts. The original stock had a scratch mark where a bear almost got him, but it was totally trashed when the troopers brought it up from under the water."

He held it up like a trophy fish.

"I saw that bastard throw it in the bay. It lay on the bottom for a few weeks but when they brought it up the ballistics matched the fragments of lead that came out of my father's brain. Now what do you want to know?"

"Why do you keep it?"

"It was his rifle. It reminds me . . ."

He turned toward the fire and held his hands over the heat and looked out at the water. Norma walked over to him and kneaded the muscles of his neck and shoulders. He bowed his head as soon as she touched him.

"It reminds me of . . . nothing."

"We watched him go to shore that night." Norma spoke into the back of his jacket.

"Hawkes had gone nuts. Papa went in to see what he could do. The weather was bad . . . blowing forty and the bottom was sandy. During the night we had to reset the anchor because we were dragging near the rocks. We saw lights in the cabin but that was all. We never heard or saw any fight. We didn't know. . . . We didn't know."

Their backs were to me and the boy with the bicycle wheel rolled into the shelter and right between us, oblivious to the distinction between inside and out.

"In the morning, he was gone. We found Hawkes ranting

about bears and voices from the center of the earth. That's when we called the troopers."

"You told the troopers you never came up on deck that night."

"So?"

That was my kind of retort. "So, now you're saying that you *were* on deck that night. Has your memory improved over time?"

Norma twisted her fingers near the nape of her neck. Lance did not look at her.

"Our memories are bad, and neither of us knows when we were on deck but we told the police the truth."

"Well, I can't help worrying about the two people who could place you on deck. But I suppose you don't have to worry. They'll both be gone for a long time."

"What people?"

"Alvin Hawkes is one."

Lance almost smiled, his lips parting as if he were thinking of taking a bite of something. "He's reliable, isn't he?"

"But at least he's alive."

"What are you talking about?"

"De De is going to be away for a long time, isn't she? Why don't you tell me about her? Then maybe I'll get out of your way."

Lance turned to me, this time more sad than angry. "Now, there's a mystery for you to solve, Younger. There's something you could do. Why don't you ask Walt Robbins how his daughter died? He's been dogging me all over the country, hinting and pushing me about De De. . . . Hell, he was down there when it happened. He knew about her married boyfriend, and that she was pregnant. But he wants to put me in the middle of it. I was seven hundred and eighty-six air miles away when she committed suicide, but he wants me mixed up in it. Why?"

"Does he think you killed her?"

His head jerked up as if he heard a twig snapping in the brush.

"She used to like me. She had a crush on me in school. Somehow, he thinks I'm to blame. But he can't think I'd kill De De."

"Were you sleeping with her around the time she died?"

I realize now that this wasn't the most tactful question. But I was still a little bent out of shape about the torque-wrench situation, and in my own cowardly way, I wanted to rap him. All my experience needling people didn't prepare me for his reaction.

Norma saw it immediately. At first she backed away but then she went to him.

"You better get out of here," she hissed at me. "I'm not kidding. You better get out of here."

She was right; one look at Lance confirmed it. He was bent double with his head buried in his hands. He was groaning in heaving breaths from a source that was some-where deeper than his stomach. His muscles were tight. He rocked on his haunches and his sister tried to murmur into his ear. His fingers were knotted together and were harden-ing into a bone white and pink fist. I knew I didn't want to be around when he got back from the place he was in.

I looked downstream and saw Edward's truck idling beside the embankment. Edward sat behind the wheel smoking a cigarette, watching. He was not making any moves, he was just watching. He could have been there forever.

Norma looked up at me. "You'd better get out of here," she repeated. "Jesus, *please.*"

I walked the sandy shore in the direction of Edward's truck. I walked slowly and didn't bolt. I could feel the force of Lance's rage. I walked slowly and tried to think good thoughts. I looked over my shoulder once and he was standing upright, his body swaying and his head cocked to the wind. His hood was down and it was a strange effect because his hands and head appeared too big compared to his body. When he saw that I was looking at him, he froze, and his sister gripped him tighter. He stood stock still. Then he shook his head as if bitten in the ear and turned suddenly and walked back into the darkness of the iron container. I moved up the slope to the truck.

The heater blasted the dusty heat of a hairdryer into my face and swirled cigarette smoke around the cab. Edward smiled and squinted at me as if I were still a long way off.

"I see you found them."

"Jesus, I almost got my dick knocked in the dirt, back there. How did you know to come here? And what were you doing anyway?" He reached under the seat and brought up a hunting rifle. A Seko stainless .375 magnum with a Bushnell scope. For walrus, charging polar bear or rhino. This was a serious piece of equipment.

"I was just thinking. You need someone to tell you a story, but I don't think that you're going to live long enough to hear it. You make people mad. Where do you want to go?"

"Somewhere I can hear a good story."

"Let me take you to Walt Robbins."

"Is he going to tell me a good story?"

"Don't know. I'll take you there to see."

TWELVE

LATER, AFTER ALL of this was over and I was sitting in the cathedral back in Sitka, I thought of that moment confronting the children and I imagined another.

I remembered reading a poem about Theodore Roethke as a child trapped up on the roof of his father's greenhouse. In my mind, I could see the boy paralyzed with fear above the adder-mouthed orchids and the steamy heat of the glass bubble. I imagined the cacophony of glass and clay pots shattering as the boy pictured himself falling to what might be his death. He conceived many stories in that moment, stories that would unravel only years later when he was a fat and eccentric old professor. Stories that would continue to unravel as he tempted insanity. I thought of a scared boy, tenuous above the beautiful and the familiar, facing a stupid, violent death.

As I said, I only thought about this much later, after I was warm and well fed. It took me some months to realize that, from the moment I rocked Toddy in my arms to the time I climbed into Edward's truck, I was perched on top of the greenhouse glass. My confrontation with the children by the river made me realize I had crawled out onto a dangerous perch. Looking down at the beautiful world I felt both light, and heavy with fear.

The sand road slid under the windshield and Edward lit a cigarette. My body bumped along like a bag of clothes. I couldn't make out the kids playing on the side of the road or the song being played on the radio. Fear, after danger has passed, has a way of making the light shimmer and my breath go shallow. Sounds take on a rounded tone, muffled and indistinct. This is fear like a sick nostalgia or a particularly bad hangover. If enlightenment feels like the top of your skull becoming infinitely large, my mind felt like a cinder.

He stopped the truck in front of a Quonset hut. There was a six-inch stovepipe jutting out of the low section of vertical wall that eventually doglegged up above the roofline. This structure had an iron roof. In fact, it was mostly iron roof. Edward turned off the key in a casually ceremonious way. I knew he wanted to talk to me.

"Talk to Walt Robbins. Don't make him mad."

"Hey, do you know something more about this than you're telling me? I mean, are you playing the mysterious guiding hand of fate or something?"

He looked at me with a dazzlingly confused look on his face.

"I don't know shit, Cecil. Talk to Walt Robbins. Okay?"

"Right."

I hopped out.

I was looking for the ravens. There were none. I was hoping to see something that would bring me luck. There was nothing. Cynicism is no protection, and the need for love does not bring luck. I had to solve this muddle on my own. I heard Edward drive away and I felt like I was standing on a distant planet. When I turned, he was already out of sight.

The Quonset hut had a nicely made front door of wooden panels that looked as if it had been rubbed with oil. There was a heavy steel door handle. The door frame was made of whitened river driftwood.

Before I could knock, Walt Robbins came to the door. "You're that investigator from Juneau. Want something to eat?"

He turned quickly and walked into the warm room. He went to the oil stove and began stirring a spoon in a big pot. "All I got's some stew. It's thin but by God it's hot."

He was maybe six two, with broad shoulders and a narrow waist. He was wearing a clean hickory shirt and black jeans. He had on wild fuzzy blue slippers that were matted with chips of wood and sand. Just as everything about Lance's body seemed to turn in, everything about Walt Robbins's body turned out. He was well muscled, but his shoulders were set loose and his arms were relaxed. His eyes were pale blue and sparkled from his face. His jaw was square, but the mouth was not tight. His hands were big, as if he could palm a water bucket and crunch it up like a pop can. He had sandy brown hair and looked like he could have crewed on any fishing boat in the Pacific.

"Got some bread. I didn't make it but it goes down

good. Want something to drink? Coffee? Something stronger?"

I was back up on the greenhouse roof. "I'm sorry. How did you know I was here? How did you know it was me?"

"Hell, man. Younger, isn't it? Where the heck do you think you are? I heard about you before you got your bags off the airplane. There's lots of room around here but this is still an awfully small town. I've been waiting for you to get here."

He handed me a bowl of stew. It looked thick and hot. He started buttering a piece of white bread. He interrupted himself and poured some whiskey into a water glass. He balanced the buttered bread on top of the glass and set it on a plywood table next to the window.

"I heard from my relatives in Juneau that Emma was steamed about someone messing around with the old woman. I heard she was flying back and forth to the home there in Sitka trying to sort it all out."

"Wait a minute. When did she make those trips? I had a friend get me the airline manifests. She wasn't on them."

He looked up at me, concerned and puzzled, like someone waking a sick baby up from a nap.

"Hell, man, she wouldn't be on the manifests. She wouldn't fly commercial to Sitka. She would fly her own plane."

"She's a pilot?"

I took a drink: warm and smoky. I felt like the cinder was soaking it up and expanding.

"She flies that plane better than most. Louis was always wanting her to do it as part of his business but she never would. Mr. Younger, there's a lot more to this than Emma wants anyone to find out."

"She seems to think the same thing about you. Her two

kids down by the river seem to want to put you in the middle of it, too."

"Those two 'kids' are meaner than pet snakes. They know something but they're never going to tell. They know something about De De and what happened in Bellingham."

He sat in a straight-back chair across the corner of the rough-hewn table. He looked at me without fear. His eyes and the features of his face were relaxed but sad, as if he had learned to live a long time with sorrow. He smiled and blue ice sparkled from deep down. I wanted to turn away but I couldn't.

"My girl's dead, Mr. Younger. She saw something, she knew something. She didn't kill herself. I don't care what anybody says. I knew about her boyfriend; I knew she might be pregnant. Hell, we fished together after her mother died, we hunted together. She was tough."

"What about her diary?"

"She was worried. I'm not saying she wasn't scared. But that last stuff. That last stuff wasn't her."

"Do you think someone else wrote it?"

"No. It's her handwriting, all right. We've written back and forth enough for me to know her writing. I think someone scared her. I think she was frightened about what was happening, what was going to happen at that trial. But she didn't kill herself."

I dished a bit of onion and moose meat into my mouth and chewed, then swallowed, grateful.

"Two things. What the hell did she see? And whatever it was, how could it be important enough for anyone to risk killing her? I mean, Alvin Hawkes was going down. Nobody, not Sy Brown or my sister, was going to make a self-defense claim fly, no matter what your daughter saw."

"Yeah, I've thought about that, too. But I don't think they—" and he nodded out the door and by that I knew he meant the brother and sister down by the river. "I don't think Lance wanted to take any chances. He is mean, Mr. Younger. He's mean but at the same time he's completely devoted to his mother and to Norma."

By the way he stopped talking I knew he was assessing how much he should trust me. We had blundered into a kind of friendship without knowing anything about the consequences. That was fine by me. In fact, I preferred it, but Walt had lost a daughter, and he was a good hunter; he knew he could never catch anything if he made too much noise. He lifted his glass to the light and looked at it as if he were appraising a gem.

"I think Lance killed her."

I let it sit there. I could tell he wasn't comfortable with the false theatrics of the pause that I was forcing between us. I also knew this guy wanted to talk. He lived alone, he was not practiced at playing these kinds of games.

"I don't understand it all, Mr. Younger; I only understand a few things. I know that my girl had a crush on Lance in school but he never looked at her twice."

"Then why would he kill her?"

"Before the trial started, De De told me she knew Louis and Hawkes had been fighting. She said that she had been on the bow of our boat checking the anchor and saw them fighting. When she told Lance about it, he got upset. She got spooked. I don't know if you've ever seen him mad—?"

I shook my head, trying not to commit.

"Well, he gets . . . crazy. De De said he got that way when she told him she'd been out on the bow that night."

"She was seen drunk down on the waterfront the day she died."

"She drank, but she was a dock rat, Mr. Younger. She had taken spills in the water as a kid; she could scramble out. She wouldn't panic and try to shinny up a piling like a drunken logger." He took my bowl and ladled out some more stew, with large slices of potatoes and a fatty piece of meat. He handed it back to me.

"Well, Emma thinks that you just want to hurt her family. She says you were passed out drunk in the fo'c'sle when you should have gone ashore with Louis. Maybe you could have prevented this whole thing."

He sat down near me again and moved closer to me than was comfortable. "You don't know how many times I've thought of that myself. If I'd been there on the beach, both of us could have handled Hawkes. She knows I've thought about it a million times. You know, Mr. Younger, maybe I could have gotten the gun and hidden it in one of the places Louis used to lock away rifles when the hunters were drinking in camp. We could have dealt with Hawkes if there were no guns lying around loose. But that's not the way it happened, and there is nothing I can do about it now."

"So why are you anxious to get into the case now?"

"I was going to let everything lie. I guess you could say I was pretty much done with the whole thing. Nothing can bring her back. Even if Lance did kill her. I thought about it a lot and no matter what, I have good memories of my girl. No matter what happens with the law or in the rest of my life, I have good memories of her."

He pointed behind his shoulder. In the back of the hut was his cot, and above it, seemingly floating on the wooden walls, I recognized a picture of a brown-haired girl holding a king salmon by a gaff hook. The girl's head was tossed back, and I could imagine the throaty laugh going out over the sunny beach. The salmon was bright silver and thick in the body.

"I have those, and no matter what else, Emma Victor doesn't have those memories. Her mind is filled with . . . I don't know what it's filled with." And he took another drink. "She talks a lot about how important her family is but I don't think she even thinks about them anymore. I mean, really thinks about them without getting angry."

"Your memories . . ."

"I was telling you. I was done with it. I was happy living here, fishing and taking out a few tourists. But then the kids came back to town and I saw them walking around and I saw them fishing the creeks, I saw them laughing and eating food at picnics. It all came back. They're alive, De De's dead. You know, it's not fair that my girl didn't have a future like these two do. But even then I didn't care that much. I just pushed it all back into my mind"—he lifted up his glass—"and into the bottle maybe a little more than before.

"Then I heard about that shooting in Sitka. When I heard that the old lady hired a detective and someone tried to kill him, I thought, well, great. Don't get me wrong. But I was happy. It meant that it was real. Does that make any sense to you? I knew this wasn't just in *my* mind. This wasn't just craziness or drinking. This was happening to someone else."

He stood up and looked down at me. "And I was happy because I counted on you looking into it. And I thought that I could help you figure it out."

"What do you have, besides instinct, to go on?"

"Nothing. But there must be something out at Prophet Cove where Louis died. I can't tell you what it is but I have a feeling that it's there."

I took a drink. "I've got to mention that you match the description of the guy who stole the rifle on the night Toddy was shot."

"Doesn't that seem just a little bit odd to you? A gun theft and the description matches me. Doesn't it point to one thing?"

My head hurt and I took another drink.

"No, it doesn't point to just one thing. There are lots of stories that could come out of this mess. Nothing, in my experience, ever points to just one thing."

"I was on a plane to Stellar the night your friend was shot. You can check my tickets."

I didn't want to check his fucking tickets. I suddenly didn't want to be there in his hut, eating good food and drinking free whiskey. The mind has a certain tolerance for confusion and ambiguity, and mine had reached its limit.

Or just about. "Tell me about Louis and Emma."

"There were some bad years. I was on the outside, but I knew Louis was not happily married."

"Did he beat his wife and kids?"

Walt looked down into the mouth of his glass. "Yeah, I think he did. You've got to understand. I loved Louis. He was my good friend. When we were young and we drank we never got in much trouble. But later, he drank when something was hurting him . . . and anger came out. Then he stopped. Those last years he was as good as I'd ever seen him." Walt swirled the whiskey around in the bottom of the glass.

I looked at Walt. The skin around his temples seemed thin, almost translucent. The weariness on his face was cut into the lines around his eyes and mouth. The Judge had been a boy who had waited all of his life to be old and venerable, but Walt was a young man whose body had grown old. His hair was thinning and flecked with gray, his skin was no longer taut over the muscles underneath. His hand didn't shake but his voice quavered slightly as he spoke.

"You can never know how a thing will turn out. I used to read to De De when she was little. Right after her bath. She wore this scratchy robe and her hair was wet and all. I'd read and let her turn the pages. She was so damn smart. Even when she couldn't read she knew when to turn the pages. You can never tell how things will turn out. I loved Louis but he wasn't all good. De De was all good but she got killed, too. I don't know how to make sense of it. I suppose I could have had things a lot better in my life. I could have done things differently, maybe. I could have avoided some bad luck. But I don't know. I don't think it would ever break down that way. She was a beautiful girl, and she was mine, and maybe that's all the luck I'll ever have in this life.

"Then there was Emma. That was good, but it was never lucky."

He looked up at me, embarrassed. "Loving a woman who is married to someone else is like winning the lottery with a forged ticket."

"Were you in love with Emma?"

"Yeah, I think I was back then."

He got up and walked around the cabin. "You ever think that memory is just a dream, Younger?"

I smiled up at him. "Most of the time."

He looked a little confused but continued. "Well, when I think about those times it really seems like a dream. Things seemed like they were always in an uproar. Louis and Emma fighting, and me trying to console them both, but really only wanting to be with Emma. I was lying to my best friend. It was not all that good a dream.

"Louis had a girlfriend who was very powerful. She was a Yupik woman with a big family. Her name was Rachel. She was different from Emma; she was quiet and strong. Louis said that being with her was like being in a safe anchorage. We all knew that as far as Em was concerned he was a lying bastard, but I think he was really in love with that Yupik woman. Just before they left Stellar there was a big confrontation, where Em called her brothers up from the lower forty-eight and they threatened Louis. It was ugly and racist, the brothers swaggering around like they were the keepers of righteousness. Nothing ever happened. They made their wishes known and left. Emma and the kids, even Louis, were no better off really. Things simmered down and Louis promised not to see Rachel, but he did on the sly for years. Before the murder, I heard that they were seeing each other a lot."

"She still around?"

Walt poured me some more whiskey and set the bottle down between us.

"Six months after Louis was killed she drowned in the river. Her skiff turned over. She was all alone, which was strange, and she hadn't packed any gear."

"What does her family say?"

"They say it's too bad she's dead. Other than that, they don't talk much to me or anyone else."

"Is Edward related to Rachel's family?"

"Your friend Edward? Yeah, I think so."

The cinder of my brain kept expanding. I had been fooled plenty of times into mistaking drunkenness for knowledge but there was a distinct edge to this feeling, an edge that led away from certainty, which made me suspect that knowledge might be behind it.

"Maybe we could go to look at the cabin. Although I'm not sure what good it would do."

"If you can get to Juneau I'll take us out to the cabin in my boat."

I heard a truck pull up and then a knock on the door. It was Hannah and she had come to pick me up.

She said we had just enough time to walk down by the river before I had to catch my plane. Hannah smiled at Walt as we stood in the doorway. She smiled and shifted from one foot to another. I knew she could smell the whiskey and she could see the glasses. She wasn't going to say anything then and I doubted she was ever going to mention it, but I knew she was not going to come in and have a drink instead of walking down by the river.

"I'll call you." I turned and extended my hand.

"Or I'll get a message through to you. Let's not wait on this thing. It's gone on long enough."

I turned and walked with Hannah to her truck. She looked down at the ground.

"Do you trust him?" she asked the tips of her boots.

"This whole case is a gray area in my brain. I don't believe or disbelieve anything, I just store it away. I tend to like him but that is all the more reason to be skeptical. He's in the gray area."

"Where am I now?" This time she asked the steering wheel.

"You? Right now you're taking me to the river."

She put the truck in gear. I felt a nervousness as Walt's hut went out of sight. Later I would recognize that as the first sounds of cracking glass above the orchids.

THIRTEEN

AS WE GOT out of the truck I held out my hand but she smiled and looked at the sand. From a plane, this section of the river would look like a twisting intestine, looping and curling back on itself. From the beach it was a series of short vistas. Curves and corners that, once rounded, revealed nothing but the river, moving and cutting away at the sandy bank. A few willows but mostly the brown water, at this point being pushed downstream, pushed by the downward slope of the mountain miles away, pushed slowly like a coasting car on the flats. There was a black and white swallow in the willow. I suppose it was telling me to be alert, to watch, to watch what was coming, but I was tired and I knew what was coming was a romantic daydream of what my life with Hannah might have been.

I remember picking berries with her in summer, behind the police academy in Sitka, in a graveyard tucked into the glen of young trees and salmonberry brambles. We walked from town late in the morning when the air was warm off the ocean and the smell of the harbor was sweet as the spray of surf. Back from the water the air was calm and the warmth radiated up from the ground. We crossed the main road that went out to the mill and walked the short gravel road down toward the graveyard. The road ran parallel to a river and the salmon were running upstream to spawn. The banks of the river were strewn with the decaying bodies of the spawned-out fish, and the air was pungent with rot. The only thing marking the entrance of the graveyard berry patch was a shoulder-high hole in the bramble where we ducked in, as if it were our childhood fort. Under the canopy of small spruce trees were the toppled markers of graves and the desiccated petals of plastic flowers.

We passed weather-worn headstones:

Anna Todd
1906–1940
Daughter-Mother

Russell Collette
1912–1944
Soldier

The sun dappled in through the canopy of the limbs and Hannah moved slowly around the graves to the edges of the clearing where the berry bushes crowded each other, reaching for the light. The berries were soft and thick with juice, loosely hung on their stems; sacks of color and flavor like eggs ripe in the bellies of the salmon running up the stream.

There were wild flowers among the graves: shooting stars, bog orchids, and the deadly monkshood.

I remember feeling I could have been underwater watching her swim naked over a tropical reef, but she was walking in and out of shadow, reaching up for the berries and gently placing them in the plastic bucket she had hung around her neck. Sometimes the upper limbs of a bramble would catch her blond hair and as she stepped forward one of them would lift a strand into the light as if it were a broken web blowing out from a doorway.

Kids had partied in the graveyard and Hannah picked up their beer cans and put them in her pack.

Tessa Malovitch
1896–1936
Committed to our Lord

Ivan Bruce
1956–1959
With the angels

I remember picking each berry. The stains on my fingers and thumb. The sweet bitter taste of the seeds resting in the back of my tongue and my teeth. I held one berry up to the light and looked at the tiny hair coming from each sack. I saw the membrane surrounding the juice as thin as the surface tension on a drop of water. An occasional horsefly would create a small disturbance in the still air and the wind would stir the trees above us, mixing the shadows in a warm broth.

We did not talk, but I could hear her humming faintly as her fingers worried over the limbs of each particular bush. It could have been a Scottish air or a sentimental dance tune. I watched her as she squatted low, working under the lower limbs to find the sweet berries near the warm ground, and then I saw her stand and stretch on her toes to reach the top of the bush. Her shirt came untucked and I saw the small of her back curve to the roundness of her thighs.

At least I think I remember seeing these things. I have a hard time sorting out memory and longing.

For instance, I wouldn't swear that we went home and I stayed sober and we made love tenderly that night, but I believe we did. I remember tasting the sun and the berries on her lips and the wind billowing through the curtains in our room as I kissed her breasts and her belly. I remember her fingers stretching against the side of my face, her saying my name over and over again. And I remember her dense taste mixing with the air, with the berries, with the memory of the sun as the darkness came on.

Walking along the river I guess I didn't care if these things really happened this way or not. I would prefer to be drunk and remember making love soberly to a woman in a memory of a truth that may have never existed, rather than suffer the certainty of an accurate recollection. These dreams that inspire loneliness are as sweet and as bitter as the seeds of berries picked in the graveyard and later found under the tongue.

She looked down and swept her hair from her face. Her shoulders rolled in the awkward, deliberate gait that goes with walking on river sand.

"Poor Cecil," she muttered. She looked up at me and I saw the curves of her face under her eyes and around her mouth. She looked younger than in our last days in Sitka. Somehow her face was softer, as if the lines, for so long taut with frustration, had relaxed. I could hear the river pushing past us and I saw an edge of the sand bank break away into the water and begin its drift toward the sound.

"You just can't leave it alone, can you? It's your sickness that has to keep moving ahead. If there is a little security and resolution in a person's life you have to come in and stir things up."

There was a mocking tone to her voice. I walked behind her a few steps and watched the swallow ruffle his feathers in anticipation of flight. He reached up under one wing with his beak, perhaps to pick at a small mite burrowing into his skin. Birds, whatever their cognitive limitations, don't have to listen to sermons from their ex-girlfriends.

"Listen, what do you want? I let you go. You packed up and walked out on Todd and me and I didn't stop you. What do you want? It seems a little late for insights."

The swallow flew, simply tipped forward and stretched, and with three strokes was out of sight beyond the curve of water and bank. A lesser woman would have thought I was picking a fight, but Hannah smiled again, and spoke out toward the water. There were slight cauliflower forms from the current blooming onto the surface.

"You act like the world isn't big enough for anything else but you. You act like when your ego swells the whole world stretches tight. Look around, Cecil, there's plenty of room. There's plenty of space left when you're around. Why don't you leave this case alone and try my way?"

I thought of that day in Sitka, standing in the wake of the door slamming. I thought of standing on the empty runway, watching the airplane bank over the sound, and I thought of geese flying overhead, an ever-widening V—away.

Of course, there is enough room in the world, but there's no use arguing with a person who has recently come to Christ. I turned and started back toward the truck by myself.

"Wait."

"I can't wait, doll. I've got to go. Listen, I've tried to feel the way you do. Even in the most watered-down form. I've tried. I sat in those community rooms and drank cup after cup of coffee and tried to accept 'a force greater than myself' but . . . I can't. . . ."

"It's because you're a man, the son of a judge."

"Bullshit. It's because there is so much happening and I spend so much of my time confused. What about "the force" between you and me, and "the force" that took a shot at Toddy. Are those the same thing? You weren't there. I held him in my arms and his chest was ripped open. You weren't there. I don't know how much room there is in the world, but there is too much fucking room when that can happen to Todd. Or that girl in Bellingham."

She looked at me and her eyes were wet. "You love mysteries so much, Cecil, I think you've made a virtue of confusion. Faith is a mystery, but you don't see that. You're like a cop when it comes to this. You only see the facts. You jump ahead to the conclusions. And then you feel empty again because you've missed the story."

The swallow landed, nearer to us. The bird was perfect in its detail. The feathers and their fishbone delicacy, the sparkle of sun on the thin liquid of its eyes. It ruffled and then tipped forward again. If its head was a cup left out, what could it be filled with?

She watched the bird. "We are free to do what we want."

"Would you stop? You're free to leave. Somebody's free to shoot Todd, and I'm free to get drunk as six hundred Indians if I want."

"There is a better way."

"I could have a lobotomy and go door-to-door with pamphlets."

She walked ahead of me, shoulders rolling, trying to hold her temper.

"You could give up the fight you are never going to win."

I stopped walking and looked down at my shoes. I had my hands in my pockets. I knew she was right, sort of. I knew I could never convince her of a truth that I couldn't define. This argument was not just about love, or about the dream that comes on after the third drink. This was about everything else: the flow of the river, and the cycle of water, Todd's shooting and my compulsive curiosity.

We both knew there was more than one force greater than me, and some of them conflict, like the one that shaped Todd and the one that wanted to kill him. These have to be at least two different things and that's okay with me. In fact, I prefer it, because for me to believe that God did this to Toddy is somehow to collude with it, to be a party to it. And that's not an option. That's crazy.

But I'd be willing, if He'd just come and take me, and that's crazy, too. Sometimes when I think about it, just for happiness, just to feel what it would be like to be a regular human, I'd surrender unashamedly. I'd live with Hannah and water my garden boxes above the channel and go to church twice a week and I'd call it heaven. But . . . I'm stuck with the world: with the rocks, with the brown water, and with the salmon that spawn, die, and drift like ghosts out to sea. I'm willing to go to the river but I can't go further, not for love, not for curiosity. I couldn't go with her because I love the river so much. I looked at Hannah and tried to imagine the words for the unimaginable faith.

The swallow appeared again and stayed perfectly still above us in the willows.

"Cecil, why do you have to be this way? Let the police figure this thing out. Stay with me and love me. I have room for you, you know."

"Just forget about Todd and De De and the rest? This whole case is just about my vanity; I give that up and you and God will take care of me?"

"Listen to yourself. The reason you do this is because you believe there is a solution out there somewhere. You have some sense of justice that requires you to find out what happened. That's faith, buster. It's twisted up, but it's faith."

She started to shake her finger at me the way the old woman in the home had done: the universal gesture of certainty.

The black and white bird lifted forward again and fell toward the water rising at the last moment to pulse along its surface with short wing strokes.

I dug my feet into the sand like a guilty little boy. The more I did it the more I became aware of it and the angrier I became.

"No," I said, and left it at that, afraid of what might come after.

The discussion ended. She was not angry or surprised by me or my answers. Then that started to irritate me. We veered to the left and walked up the steep sandy embankment to a fringe of firm but unstable ground. Hannah went first, and when we cleared the top we both stopped and looked over the tundra. In its expanse it was abstract, but up close it was crowded with detail: the bunched moss and the thin clumps of grass, a ptarmigan's gray mottled feather tucked under a hillock and the thin tracings of a rabbit track going away from the river. Then, unexpectedly, she turned to me and took my hands in hers. She was crying. The tears were like crystals in the brief light. She rubbed her mittened hands over the red skin of my bare knuckles.

"You think that I'm stupid. You think that I'm too weak to live with these 'heroic' contradictions that you live with. And you think that I don't love you. But that's not true. None of that is true. You built the barrier, not me. Not faith, not your father, but you. And you know that's true."

"It could well be true. . . ." I felt my anger rise and disappear above the river. I brushed her hair away from her eyes and moved the back of my hand against her cheek. "But I can't recognize the truth until I know exactly where I am."

She hugged me. Even through her thick coat I could feel the muscles running down her back tense in quick powerful spasms. She snuffled on the back of my collar and planted a quick kiss on my ear and then she whispered, "This isn't all about you, you know."

"I know," I said and we walked toward the truck.

FOURTEEN

WE DIDN'T SPEAK as she drove me to the airport. In the
parking lot I bought a pint of Kentucky bourbon for $25
from a cab driver who had religious medals hanging from
his rearview mirror.

Edward was there at the single gate and he smiled as I
went toward the plane, and then he walked over to me. He
put his arms on my shoulders and then looked down at the
ground.

"There is a story about a human being who marries a
bear. Maybe you should hear it."

"How does it end?"

"Depends."

I looked at him and squinted. "You, too? What are you,
running for office? You're not making sense."

"It depends on where you are. It depends on who the bear
is."

"I don't know what the fuck you're talking about."

He smiled. And his eyebrows arched in the circle that
completed the curve of his cheekbones. "Be careful, Cecil.
You are going to drink. But don't ruin your luck."

"I'll try. Don't listen to me. It's somebody else talking."

"Okay."

We shook hands and I turned and climbed the stairs to the plane. I leaned against the window and watched Hannah walk with Edward back to his truck. I opened the bottle and drank deeply. There is something ardent and romantic about getting drunk. I feel like it's a homecoming and a departure all at once.

I am sitting in the central tube of a riveted aluminum spear, being driven deeper and deeper into my seat as we lift off the runway and then, as we ease up and bank over the south, I am astride a trumpeter swan gliding easily along the currents of subarctic air.

I don't want to, but I force myself to take six long swallows to finish the bottle so the flight attendant will not think I'm rude or hiding anything when she offers me a drink. Somehow there is music, a string section playing "Norwegian Wood" above the constant grinding drone of the Rolls-Royce engines. The pressure builds up behind my eyes and my head begins to feel slightly unhinged from my neck. I plug my nose and blow out. Air gushes out of my ears and new sounds flood in. The liquor cart is being unfolded and the blond flight attendant with the purple mascara bangs it gently on the bulkhead and I hear the sweet tinkle of the tiny bottles.

Taking hallucinogenic drugs is very much like taking a trip: leaving one place and going to another. But getting drunk is like hiring a sitter and staying in. There are no lightning blasts of clarity or luminous burning bushes, but only the vague warm sentimentality that seeps in around the edges like the sliding chords of a steel guitar. The back of my throat and the bottom of my stomach fill with iron filings, and I feel the pressure of my peripheral vision narrowing.

The plane climbed through the cloud cover and we poked into the uniformly sunny world of high altitude. The cart was loaded and happily jingling down the aisle. I was by the window and the woman on the aisle heaved a long breath and said to herself and to me: "Thank God we're out of that hellhole."

She was white and wearing a crisp business suit, straight navy skirt, pleated white blouse, and oversized amber trade-bead necklace. Her fingernails were manicured to shapely clear talons. She clenched and unclenched her fingers as we rose to cruising altitude.

"To what do you owe the good fortune of getting out of Stellar?" She looked at me and her eyes seemed to be gay as paper lanterns at a country picnic.

"It was time to go," I said.

"Exactly!" And she thumped the padded armrest with her fists. Her silver bracelets tinkled briefly as the liquor cart pulled abeam and I bought her a scotch and soda. I had bourbon. We talked about something inane and I had a sense she knew it was inane as well. We were talking out of tension, and all the while I kept thinking about Hannah and

Toddy and that dismal avocado in the salad. My seatmate was a CPA and I remember her saying that she didn't use a pencil and she "did cities and not books."

I smiled a knowing kind of grin like I knew what she was talking about and had turned it into some sort of double entendre.

She was glad to be leaving Stellar because she was afraid she was going to get stuck there for weeks trying to sort out the books for the city.

"These are Stone Age people, for Christsakes. Not that they are to blame, I suppose, but they don't have any real notion about fiscal responsibility. They don't understand the . . . the . . ." She traced a perfectly shaped nail down the tip of her nose to her tongue. "—The substance of good accounting."

I was chewing that one over when we hit an air pocket and nervous laughter rose from all the passengers. The cabin was growing dark now and the reading lights were coming on. Thick-bodied travelers jiggled in their seats. Strapped in. Some were asleep with their mouths open in corpulent repose. We were all hurtling through the air at 450 miles per hour inside a pressurized aluminum tube. Far below I imagined the sound of our engines falling on a bull moose. He might have startled and lifted his head slightly.

I dimly remember changing planes in Anchorage. I remember trying to convince my racist accountant friend to come with me to the Baranof Hotel in Juneau or to the Red Dog Saloon. I remember the angry expression of some large white man with folded arms who had apparently come to meet her at the airport. I remember the tinge of potential violence in the air or maybe it was the edge to someone's voice.

I don't think that I got into a fight.

I slept and drank from Anchorage to Juneau and I stole bottles off the cart when I walked back to the coffin-sized bathroom. The flight was continuing to Seattle, and there were three people in tweed coats and rubber shoes waiting in the Juneau airport.

Someone offered me a joint in a bathroom, maybe in the airport, and I turned it down. I remembered three years ago I had sworn to a sixteen-year-old girl that I would never smoke pot without her and we would only do it in the Pike Place Market in Seattle. This sworn oath is clearer now than any moment of the plane ride. I sat down on the toilet in the airport bathroom and put my head in my hands.

I'd been looking for a guy in Seattle, and thought he worked at one of the fish stands. He might have been a witness to a boat fire in Ketchikan the fall before. I met her in the morning on the corner near the bus stop where the tattoo parlor used to be. She had short black hair and she offered to keep me company. She had two joints in a plastic soap case that looked like it was stuffed with her important papers. We smoked the joints slowly and intermittently at various points around the market. We squatted by the green pillars and listened to Baby Gramps play "Teddy Bears' Picnic" on his steel guitar. We watched the men throw salmon over the counter to be weighed, and laughed when they dropped them, slippery and comic like an old movie. The fish were beautiful silver swimmers, split down the middle, their red flesh flashing like a starlet's lips.

We kissed on the balcony over the waterfront. We watched tourists shuffle around the panhandlers, and we ate calamari and baklava sitting by the window in an upstairs café, trying to guess where all the ships were bound for. We stepped out into the sunshine and her skin was a golden slippery pink, like a little girl in her first two-piece bathing suit. We drank coffee and white zinfandel. An old man dressed like a logger did silly and obvious sleight of hand, but she laughed and put change in his hat.

She had a few belt buckles made from elk horn that she was going to sell but she had given them to a friend to keep and he had traded them off for a pizza and a bottle of apple wine, which he at least offered to share with us, but we declined.

At six o'clock we kissed by the stainless steel flower bins that were empty except for the bright blue and red smear of petals across the bottom. A bus blew the pages of a magazine across Pike Street in the wake of its exhaust. There were long shadows toward midtown. A Chinese man squatted by one of the green pillars and knocked spit out of his harmonica.

We bought fresh raspberries and shrimp and tried to cook the shrimp over a barrel fire on the waterfront, but the wood was soaked in creosote and the shrimp turned to tar. She ate raspberries and cried. She cried until her mascara ran like the water stains under a roof spout. It was the snotty, awkward crying of a child, and I held her and kissed the top of her head and promised.

She had a theory about unhappiness. She let herself be really unhappy a little every day, and that way she would not save it up for when she was old. She said she would never end up like her mom. She told me this and she wiped her nose on her sleeve. We finished the last of the joint and the raspberries and we burned the shrimp. Then I drove her out to her aunt's house in Woodinville, where the yard was matted down and muddy, with a pit bull chained to an outboard motor in the corner. Bugs swarmed the porch light. Her aunt turned the TV down when we knocked, but stayed sitting on the couch. We kissed good-bye and I promised to meet her at the market the next day. But when I saw her she snubbed me. I think she had gotten into some kind of trouble because there was the crescent of a fresh bruise under her makeup. I waved and she smiled faintly and turned her back.

Later I heard from a guy who knew her uncle in jail that she'd hung herself in a halfway house on the Olympic Peninsula. I never got any more details but I didn't disbelieve the rumor. My father told me that the first rule of unhappiness is that you can accept the way things are, or change. As long as you live drunk or with an acceptable daily level of unhappiness, you can avoid this rule altogether. But some people find that no matter what they do, unhappiness is cumulative. Some people mistreat their lovers and stay drunk so they can live the exclusive romance that's found in memory and cheap sentiment.

I was sitting in an airport bathroom thinking about my own theory of unhappiness. I had this idea that if someone would only love me with enough conviction and if I could understand just what the fuck the "substance of good accounting" was, everything would come clear.

I tried to add things up: There was a hole in Toddy's back

the size of a softball. There were papers and reports and photographs about a murder that didn't add up to a story. There were Lance and his sister, both less than forthcoming, but then I was a lot less than worth coming forth to. Emma Victor with her tight smile and milky stare. Louis Victor dead and eaten by the bears. De De flopped like a rag doll on a pier in Bellingham and Walt Robbins with his earnest faith in his daughter. And in the midst of this there was someone trying to kill me before I got to something that I couldn't at this point even imagine existed. I tried to add it up, and I couldn't understand the substance of good accounting. I was rocketing around in one pressurized tube after another, with facts swirling around me like mosquitoes.

The Juneau airport shines with etched glass and makes you think you've really arrived in a city. I sat in the bar and looked out over the highway and I could see the lights of the department stores and video shops nestled under the lip of the glacier. The glacier has a massive presence like the sound of a bear ahead of you in the brush. I drank and twisted my napkin into a knot. Someone asked me about Toddy and I talked about my father. I remember getting angry and I remember thinking about getting something to eat. Someone, perhaps another large white man with folded arms, suggested that I go downtown. A cabbie fronted me the fare. I don't know why.

It was raining hard and I stood under a theater marquee for ten minutes until I saw someone I thought I knew and we walked the bars. I remember stuffed animal heads and a woman in a tank top with a bloody nose. I remember a waitress dropping an entire tray of drinks and I think I remember someone playing the saxophone out in the rain on the dock by the big mural of the raven. Warm rain, I thought, and a fried food smell up from the vents. Behind me the mountain was a tangle of trees and stone and quick little rivulets running into iron culverts rolling under the streets.

On the edge of town the empty mines were quiet, the rocks piled like empty shells in the middens. Rain and the salt breath of the tide flats. Whiskey and popcorn. Coffee, sour and bubbling like thermal mud in the urn at the shelter. The boys sleeping at the bus stop were wearing two sets of clothes. Billy was dancing in the street and flashing his Indian money around, his grandma bundled up and leaning on her cane under the bus-stop roof. Billy doing an old dance, Billy muttering in drunken Tlingit. His grandma, sober and watchful, too wise to be really ashamed but too old and tired not to be hurt by his foolishness.

There was a fire in a trash bin behind one of the hotels and a bottle being shared. I remember landing on the sidewalk in front of the lawyers' bar. Diamonds on the slick cement sidewalk. I remember angry voices and Billy chanting and yelling just out of hearing. I remember hands on the back of my jacket, pulling me up as I was lying facedown. I think I was choking. Long flight of stairs inside a brown stairwell. Popcorn again and a booming woman's voice coming up from below as if she were in the back of a cave, music swelling and sirens, squealing tires and music, dance music, and popcorn and sour butter, salt, and jostling up the stairs, looking at the weave of mildewed carpet and row after row of cracked brown door frames.

It was about 9:00 A.M. when I woke up. Someone had thrown some sofa cushions on the floor and my face was crushed down in the crack between them. I felt like I had an anvil on the back of my neck. I was able to turn my head and see two Indian men sitting on a couch without cushions. They were wearing brown canvas work clothes and one was wearing a baseball cap. The other was fidgeting with his lighter and balancing a cup of coffee on his knee. The TV was on and there was some commotion in the bathroom. The one with the coffee cup turned to his companion.

"Where's Auntie?"

"She's in the bathroom ragging on Calvin about how he's butchering his deer. She says he shouldn't have it in the bathtub."

They stared out toward the bathroom and then down at me.

"Who's he?"

"Some guy that Auntie wants to talk to."

Calvin came out of the bathroom. He was wearing a flannel shirt with the sleeves rolled up. His hands were bloody, and in one of them he was carrying a hunting knife with a curved blade. He had shoulder-length black hair and his eyes were sparkling.

"You got a better stone than the one in the kitchen? I dulled this blade on the hair, and she wants it boned out just right."

"Yeah, I'll take a look."

The hatless one stepped over me to the alcove that had been the kitchen. There was a counter with a gap of darkened wallboard where the dishwasher had been. There was a camp stove set up on the countertop. There was a roll of butcher paper, scissors, tape, and a felt-tip pen. The hatless one rummaged in the drawers. Calvin bent down over me and smiled.

"You really disappoint me, man."

His breath was in my face. It was warm and smelled sweet, like bacon. I tried to sit up, without luck. My head felt like a collapsing melon. I lay back down. He squatted down next to me on the floor and stared at me, grinning.

"I've been studying white people for years, and I am bitterly—I mean bitterly—disappointed." He gestured toward the TV. "Look on television. Private detectives are not supposed to be like this. You people are supposed to be in charge! You are supposed to have a cool apartment and a fast car. Man, you are supposed to be following beautiful women and making deals. I mean, what I see of you guys on television and what I've got here now are . . . inconsistent."

The hatless one came back toward us. "Hey! Here." He handed Calvin a rectangular piece of marble, smooth on one side and rough on the other.

"Yeah, thanks." He looked back down at me. "And look at you . . . drunk. I see so many of your people drunk. It must be the pain of running the world. Is that it, Kemosabe? The pain of running the world? I mean, I'm smart enough to know that you don't walk around like pilgrims with three-cornered hats and big buckles and shit. I've seen TV, man. I know what you are supposed to be, but you . . . you're a mess. Where did Auntie find you anyway?"

I looked up at him and he was still smiling sweetly.

I made it up on one elbow and said, "I *am* fucking in charge. Just tell me where I am, who you are, and if I have a broken nose or not."

He laughed loudly and patted my head as if I were a favorite pup. "Just so, man. Just so. I don't think your nose is broke."

A familiar old woman's voice came from the bathroom. "Calvin, bring that knife back in here."

"Just stay here, she wants to talk to you."

"Okay, but I need to use the bathroom."

Now he frowned. He took a long breath as if he were amazed at his own patience with me. "Auntie, can we get in the bathroom a minute?"

I heard an muttering back out of the bathroom and disappear down a hallway. I made my way to my feet and stood still for a second. I had been in these apartments before. They were above the movie theater and the café. The window was open a crack and the vent for the café was a few feet underneath. I could clearly smell fried potatoes. Out past the vent I could see the flat roofs puddled with rainwater along the old buildings of Front Street, and I could see the mountains of Douglas Island. I heard the television and the grinding chug of the garbage truck in the alley. I heard breaking glass and someone yelling at a busboy in Spanish. There was a raven on a TV antenna ten feet from the window and an eagle drawn out wide and gliding over the channel.

I walked to the bathroom and opened the door. There was a deer hanging from the shower nozzle, with its hind legs resting in the tub. It was a buck. He was hanging by a cord knotted around his neck. His head and horns were intact and the hide was lying in the tub, puddled at his feet as if he had undressed to take a shower. His head was cocked at that impossible angle of a hanging death, and his tongue lolled out the side of his mouth. The hair on his delicate head and ears was fine and soft brown in comparison to the white

sheen of the layer of fat that covered his exposed musculature. His chest was split open and cleaned out. His eyes
were black opaque marbles.

Calvin stood behind me. "We got him over on Admiralty.
Brought him back on my uncle's skiff. Auntie came from
Sitka and wants to take some back with her and I was going
to give the rest to her family."

"You going to can him or freeze him?"

"I think we're going to eat him tonight or the next day. I
don't know. Listen, you're just going to wash, right? I mean you
can't do anything else in here with him, you understand. Just
wash and wash up good and don't touch anything."

I heard an old woman's voice croak behind him. "Calvin,
get back in there and bone that deer out. I want to take some to
the Home. Mr. Younger, come with me into the other room."

Calvin stood aside and I saw Mrs. Victor in her wheelchair. Her fists knotted around the rims of her wheels and
her jaw jutted up at me. Now my stomach was a dark burrow
of sleeping animals again and I turned white at the thought
of how bad my case had become.

"One second."

I washed my face. The bathroom was clean, and there
were clean towels, blue and pink, on the rack. The tile was
coming off around the tub and the toilet ran continually but
there was hot water. I gingerly washed around the fresh scab
on my nose and I examined myself for any other damage. I
tried to pull myself together. I tucked my shirt in. I was both
drunk and hung over at the same time: self-conscious and
queasy but still a little spinny. These are the times that one
makes the meaningless promises to stop drinking. But I was
old enough to know better.

I went into the bedroom. There was a stool and a cot set

up in the corner. Mrs. Victor positioned her chair in the middle of the room and rolled around to face me.

"Do I pay you for your hours in the bars?"

"No, ma'am."

"What have you found?"

I briefly considered telling her how sick I was, thinking that would illustrate the state of the case, but I knew I was being selfish. I sat on the stool and rocked from one cheek to the other. My mind was blank. It was like snorkeling a hundred miles offshore, looking down into the ocean and seeing only the gray-green screen of deep water with the corona of the sun marking a big zero in every direction that I looked. Then a few thoughts swam by.

"Your grandchildren are angry, and Walt Robbins thinks that they know more than they are telling."

"Yes."

"Your daughter-in-law is lying to me and I don't know why."

She nodded her head, continuing to stare.

"And someone is trying to kill me, but he is not very direct. And that tells me that he is a thoughtful person and not just crazy mean."

"Is that all?"

I nodded and looked down at the old scabs on my fingers. She took another breath and spoke slowly to me as if English were my second language.

"Do you know about the trouble in my son's family?"

"Some of it. Do you?"

"Some of it. It had to do with a girlfriend and Louis being too . . . too . . . mannish."

She rolled closer to me, almost touching my knees with hers.

"Walter Robbins called me yesterday and told me you were coming and he told me that you would be drunk. He told me to get you cleaned up to meet him on the city dock. Last night my nephews found you out on the street and brought you here. I flew to Juneau to talk to you. Walt will be here today."

"I don't know that much. I'm sorry but it's a wasted trip. I don't know what you can talk to me about."

She lifted a finger as if to begin drawing a picture in the air. Her eyes were focused somewhere behind my head.

"I used to tell all of my children and my grandchildren this story. It was told to me by my father's people in Yakutat. My uncles told it to me. It is a true story. I know you will not believe it is a true story. White people do not believe these stories. Just try and listen."

Calvin and the hatless one came into the room and Calvin gave me a cup of coffee and then they both sat down on the floor with their backs to the wall looking up at their auntie.

"A long time ago there was this girl. She had brothers. Her brothers were good hunters and they never were hungry. The girl walked a long way away to pick berries and bring them back to her brothers and they were happy with her. This girl married a brown bear. She met him in the berries and the brothers did not know about him. She would go out and meet him and they would pick berries together. This girl married the bear and just about the time she was becoming a woman she moved away from the village and did not tell everything to the brothers. The brothers were not so happy but the girl would still bring them berries and they would eat.

"She loved the bear and they had two babies that were . . . I don't know . . . kind of half-bear and half-people.

183

These babies could pick berries and hunt and these babies were good fishermen, too. Their uncles never knew about them but they were curious about their uncles. When they got older and older they began to hunt closer to their uncles' village. One day the uncles saw the bear-human babies. The babies ran and told the girl. The girl told her husband. This girl, she loved her husband so much. The husband said that they had to move their den farther away from the village. This girl—she was so pretty. She cried and cried and said that she did not want to live far away from the village. Her husband said that if she would not leave their den he would go back to his bear wife because it was not safe for him there. He told her he was going to go hunting. He asked her to pack all of their baskets and blankets and he would come back for them later.

"Then the bear went hunting. This bear was big, and a good hunter, too. After this bear went hunting the girl called her babies inside and asked them if they loved their father, this bear. She told them to wait for him to come back from hunting. To wait for him down on the white sandy beach. To wait on the sandy beach and when he came back they were to kill him. They were to eat him and put his skin out on the rocks so the uncles would find him and know the bear was not hunting near the village. The babies listened to their mother, this girl who was so pretty—and when their father came back from hunting they did just like she said. And they ate him and laid his skin out on the rocks for their uncles."

She placed her hands down to her sides. Calvin took a drink of his coffee and cleared his throat. I kept staring down at my old scabs. She looked at me with sympathy and a little disgust.

"I knew you wouldn't believe it. No matter what you tell a

white person it all goes to the same place. Get yourself something to eat and go to the dock before noon. And, Calvin, get that deer boned out."

She turned on the radio and I knew from that my audience was over. She turned and looked at me one last time.

"I will see you in Sitka," she said.

FIFTEEN

THE MOUNTAINS WERE staring down at me like my
parents. My head hurt so much I couldn't tell if I actually
saw them or was vividly dreaming in the process of waking
up.

I was sitting on the bull rail of the municipal dock in
Juneau staring out to the Gastineau Channel with a cup of
coffee in a paper cup in one hand and a toasted onion bagel
in the other. Miraculously, my duffle bag with my clothes
and papers was sitting on the dock. I was dangling my feet
about fifty feet above the water, and a raven was staring at
me as if he were from the Temperance League. I had no
clear memory of the events of last night and of the days
before. In the foreground was Mrs. Victor in her chair and
the story of the woman who married a bear. I also knew with
what felt like an emerging certainty that I was supposed to
meet Walt Robbins here. Meet Walt, meet Walt, that was
clear. It was not just an appointment but some sort of
imperative. I was still struggling with a new form of accounting but I kept running into the exposed blade of my
headache.

It was not raining, but the air was thick with moisture. There was a swirl of cloud in the middle of the channel that rested ten feet from the surface. The cloud moved slowly in wisps, floating on the imperceptible waves of heat radiating off the water. It moved in on itself and away; it was translucent, and when the sun broke briefly from the mountains on Douglas Island it rose in a curtain of mist and disappeared into the dense atmosphere of water and light. I thought of a roomful of silken veils, and Hannah dancing as the heat began to rise. There was a curtain beaded with glass crystals and a tropical wind swirling through the room. There was a glass of milk on a long bench and Dizzy Gillespie was lifting his horn to his lips. I watched him close his eyes and pucker way down in his weird distended, bullfrog neck, then I heard the blast of a boat's signal horn cutting through my dream and I saw Walt Robbins's troller coming through the mist to tie to the lower floating dock. Walt was in the wheelhouse and was waving to me to come down the ramp and prepare to take in the bow line.

I looked around for someplace to set my bagel. I stared at the raven, gave up any thoughts of guile, and offered it to him. He took half and stepped off the dock into a clumsy, heavy flight, alighting on a lower piling where he ripped into the bagel like a bear into a salmon, chuckling and cackling, apparently to himself.

I balanced my coffee down the ramp and made it to the edge of the dock about the same time the *Oso* did. The diesel engine was thrumming at low RPMs. About six feet from the edge of the dock, Walt put the drive train into reverse and gently eased the boat in. He came out the side door of the wheelhouse onto the narrow deck and threw the bow line the two feet to me. He gestured toward the forward cleat. He then went directly to the stern, grabbed a line and hopped onto the dock, took a wrap on the cleat, and slowed the boat to a stop as I began to tie the bow line.

"My God, but you look rough, son."

"Not so bad. When do we have to pull out? Do I have time to make some calls?"

"I guess you can make any calls you want. But we have to get going to make the best tide."

The *Oso* was an old-style troller with a small wheelhouse that was bolted onto the massively built wooden hull. It was bolted on so that if it was swept away in green water the hull would be mostly intact and the small hole could be plugged. The stern was long and swept under to the waterline where she was driven by one propeller. The engine sat amidships right next to the deckhand's bunk. It was small and dark inside the hull. The oak ribs and the cedar planks were unpainted and deeply stained with the carbon of diesel stoves and years of oil lamps burning at the heads of the bunks. This was a workboat: a floating tractor. Not built for romance, but now romantic in its old age.

"I've got what gear you'll need below: boots and such. I don't want to rush you, son, but I think we really should be going."

"Okay. Just one thing."

I turned and set my cup down on the bull rail and walked up the ramp again. There was a man in a clear plastic raincoat speaking to a woman in German. They were trying to frame a picture of the *Oso* to include me as I walked up the dock. The closer I came, the further back the man moved until finally he stumbled and nearly fell backward. The woman gestured wildly and said something that sounded like a command to him in German.

I went to the pay phone, called the hospital in Sitka, and asked after Todd. Fluids, infection, fever. If the fever didn't go down by tomorrow they were going to have to go in again and irrigate the wounds. I hung up.

Then I called Duarte and asked him if he would take Toddy's fish tank over to the hospital and I asked him to check the house to make sure the windows weren't leaking around the frames, and to pick up my mail. Duarte was grouchy that I'd waked him up, and he acted at first like I had asked him to dig the Panama Canal, but he lightened up when he figured he would get a shot at my refrigerator. I hung up.

The German man was inexplicably trying to get another shot of me, and his wife now had a tissue in her hand.

I felt okay about asking Duarte to run errands for me. If he said he was going to do something I could count on it. It was the things he didn't mention that I had to worry about.

I made one last call to a friend at the Sitka flight service and asked her to double-check some things. I dug into my pack and looked through the file and found the phone records from Emma Victor's house on the night Todd was shot. There was no record of a call to my house on that evening.

I turned from the pay phone and bumped squarely into George Doggy's chest.

"You're looking rough, Younger."

"You're looking very large, Doggy. What the hell are you doing standing on my shoelaces?"

"Younger, I heard that you were around and I thought I just *had* to see you."

"I got a boat to catch, Doggy. Listen, I'm staying out of trouble. Unless this is official."

"Oh no, nothing official. A citizen turned up last week and said you stole some of his money and threw him down the stairs for sport."

"A misunderstanding."

"I also heard that this same citizen was supposed to get a wad of cash for shooting you with a large-caliber handgun. And he didn't collect until someone dropped at least part of it by the hospital."

"Can you beat that? I've got to go."

"Listen, Younger, I'm sorry about getting on you like I did at the hospital. I . . . hell, I'm not going to try and be nice to you, it's just I've got something you should see."

He handed me some papers and I recognized forms from the Sitka Police Department.

"It's the police reports on the gun theft. Do you want to guess who the witness was?"

I shook my head.

"Giving phoney names can backfire, if someone sees you or you need to backtrack on your story. The Sitka witness used her real name because she was afraid someone in town would recognize her. It was Emma Victor."

I looked down at my shoes. Again, I was trying to think of some dazzling quip to let Doggy know that I fully understood the implications and was on top of everything.

"Wow. Whaddaya think?"

"I don't know, for certain. But Emma Victor isn't at her home, and neither is her plane. I know that you and Robbins have something cooking and you're going out to the cabin in Prophet Cove. I thought I'd warn you that it's possible you're going to have company."

"Do you know what Walt and I have cooking?"

"No. But I want you to tell me."

I grabbed Doggy by the shoulders and swung him around toward the water. I put my right arm around him and yelled over to the German couple, "Picture. Picture." The man immediately lifted his camera to his face and snapped one. Then he waved a clumsy wave of appreciation and said, "Very good photo—very handsome" as I turned and walked down the ramp.

"Be careful, Younger. I'm retired. I don't need any more business. Particularly if you wash up on some beach somewhere."

I waved over my shoulder. "Very good photo—very handsome." I didn't look back to watch him go.

Walt had the bow line untied and was standing at the stern holding the line looped around the cleat. I had a sense that it wasn't only the tide that rushed him. He was staring inward and down at the water. His jaw moved slightly as if he were grinding his teeth. He was untying an emotional knot that had been cinched tight years ago. He was working, working it, his mind and his hands rubbed raw by the effort.

As I walked down the ramp he gestured for me to hold the stern line and he made ready to go to the wheel. Walt was a man comfortable in motion, and knots, hard implacable knots, irritated him like a drop of gasoline in the eye. I waited until he was at the wheel and put my weight against the hull. I pushed away from the dock and stepped high up onto the gunnel. She was perhaps fifteen tons of dead weight but she floated free of the dock like an airborne seed. I looked to the wheelhouse. Walt was scanning the channel, and although he was tapping his foot he didn't appear to be grinding his teeth.

It was going to be a ten-hour run to the hunting cabin near Prophet Cove. The clouds were low and the water would be smooth, at least until we rounded the point and turned to the west. If I was going to get any rest, the smooth water was the time to get it. Walt gave me earplugs and headphone ear protectors and still the sound of the engine near the crew bunk vibrated my blood vessels. I wadded my coat under my head and pulled a sleeping bag over my legs and closed my eyes.

These morning naps can bring vivid dreams, but on that morning the motion of the boat and the constant grinding of the engine slipped me into a blurred atmosphere. I floated on the thin surface, and below there was a dark world of tiny-eyed crustaceans. I only had a vague sense of the blooms of the algae and euphausiids, clouds of nutrient with droplets of herring and drifts of salmon, but I could feel their presence as if they were restlessly tapping on the hull of the *Oso* to remind me to stay awake, stay awake.

"Wake up, son. You better take a look at this."

I had no idea how long I had slept but the engine was idled down and the drive train was out of gear. I climbed the ladder to the cramped wheelhouse. Walt had a cup of tea in his hand and he gestured out the side door.

"Go forward and look about twenty feet off at two o'clock."

"Is everything okay?"

"Yeah, just go take a look."

I wasn't completely sure if this was a prank, a test, or more of the dream seeping into my awakening. I ducked my head and went forward by the anchor winch. I squatted down and looked out at two o'clock.

The *Oso* was two hundred yards offshore and I could see the lead gray rocks blend to the mat of moss and spruce and hemlock forest. There were three eagles perched in the trees, scanning the water. I turned around and looked at Walt and he smiled and nodded back. Eagles? I thought. He woke me up to show me some fucking eagles? I looked back toward the shore. There were quite a few gulls and I noticed four sea lions curling through the water. Then about ten feet from the hull I saw a bubble the size of a cantaloupe break onto the surface and then another and another, arching out into a circle toward the shore.

I never feel my body in my dreams, it's as if I have no biology in my subconscious. In my dreams my emotions are—just there—in the atmosphere of the dream, like rain or background radiation. One good clue that I'm not dreaming is when my body sends me specific messages. As I watched the bubbles start to close in a perfect circle about forty feet across I could feel the hair standing up on the back of my neck. My breath was short and my eyes started to tingle.

An almost subsonic groan percolated up from below and the surface of the water broke. Giant ovoid forms heaved up out of the water, abstract at first, ten feet of curve, texture, and confined space. The water boiled with little silvery fish dense on the surface like a trillion dollars in quarters spilling onto a sidewalk. Then, the surface of the water actually bent as the huge bulk continued to rise and the two forms closed together combining into one, slippery gray-black monument. There was something familiar at this point, and my mind began to condense around a recognition. There was a massive exploding breath and the damp smell of fish and tideflat; a cloud of vapor drifting away. As the form tipped to the side and lay in the water, a narrow rubbery wing lifted out of the sea and slapped the surface: curved and scalloped, knobby and limber. It popped the water and the form lengthened as it tipped to the plane of the horizon, as if it spilled out of itself. Then, an eye, an eye the size of a softball. And it's not until you see the eye that the parts, the forms, become whole, and the realization wells up that this is an animal, a warm-blooded creature whose heart pumps gallons of blood a stroke and whose eyes see as you are seeing, whose lungs exhale as you are exhaling now, relaxing with the return to familiar form. Whale. Humpback whale, feeding on herring.

There were two whales idly swimming toward the southern point of the beach. They traveled slowly. They threw their flukes to the surface and dove slowly. Then, in moments, one of them would begin to blow the ring of bubbles that, as they rose to the surface, acted like a net bunching the herring up. Both whales would then move up underneath the ball of herring with their mouths open, gathering them in and herding them against the surface. After they broke the surface and snapped their jaws shut, they strained the water out through their baleen and swallowed the herring.

After we'd watched about four dives Walt put the engine in gear and raised the RPMs. He went back to his course and I moved around the deck. There was a raft of old-squaw ducks sputtering along behind the whales, picking up on the herring that were stunned on the surface. The sea lions looped through the brine of fish and ducks to scavenge their fair share. The two whales left vapor clouds on the surface and I turned my back to them and walked into the wheelhouse.

Back inside, Walt didn't mention the whales, he just looked down at the chart and steered toward the new compass heading. He was smiling. I watched the steam from the kettle on the oil stove flutter as the *Oso* swayed into her new course. The whales would feed all summer long and then be off to warm water for the breeding season. I was thinking about where I might be next spring.

Once we were steady on the new course, Walt set the automatic pilot, leaned back from the wheel, and looked at me.

"You think she knows about what we're up to?"

"You mean Emma? I don't know. I've been going round and round about that. I've got some people at the flight service checking out some names for me. She flies a plane. If she tells me that she can't, then that will make me worry. I want to know if she's filed flight plans coming in and out of Sitka. If she was up to something, I doubt that she filed any plans at all."

"She loves her children, and you know it's crazy, but she loved Louis," Walt said. "She was fierce in the way she loved him. Fierce. Almost like anger, she loved him so much."

"The night Todd was shot she called me, but not from her house. She may not be the killer but she knows something. She knows something about her husband's death. What do you think? Could she have flown in, killed him and flown away in her airplane, without anyone ever suspecting?"

"I don't know. Emma is odd. I used to hold my breath around her. Sometimes when I was standing close to her I just found my hand coming up and moving over to touch her.

Just my hand—like I couldn't do anything about it. I would move away from her but that was no good. I would be reading a magazine or listening to the radio and I would find myself stopped, just looking at the pages and thinking about her. I think I loved her so much sometimes I wanted to wrap her around me like an animal skin. But I don't think I know her."

He was embarrassed. He stood at the wheel apparently listening to something. Then he came back. I handed him his tea.

"What about the old lady, Louis's mother. She acts like she knows everything. Do you think she does?"

Robbins tilted his head toward me and smiled. "The old lady knows a hell of a lot. I've had a feeling for a long time that she knows everything, but then—she could just know the end of the story and want us to fill in the rest."

He put down his tea. "You want something to eat?"

We ate sandwiches and drank milk out of heavy white mugs that had circular coffee stains in the bottom. Periodically, he gave me a new course to steer and I watched the compass and turned the adjustments on the automatic pilot to match the numbers that he gave me. We were moving to the southwest now. The mountains came down steeply to the beach and as the thin fall light began to fail, the forests appeared thick and textured like the folded robes of a sitting monk. A thin trail of diesel exhaust spindled out behind us and dissipated with the long wake of the vessel, stretching in the widening V.

It was dark by the time we finished setting the anchor in Prophet Cove. On the outline of the shore I could make out the haze of alder branches and leaves scattered on the tufted beach fringe. After setting the anchor Walt turned off the engine; the quiet at first rushed into my ears and then spread out across the water. On shore there was a slight swell, and the rocks hissed as it broke gently on the beach. Walt lit a kerosene lamp and turned off the two electric bulbs near the lower berths. I stood on deck and peed out into the water. Two mergansers paddled by: watchful— watchful—their bills darting like an ant's antenna, and I could see the white head of an eagle perched on the low overhanging branch of an alder tree.

Set in from the beach fringe, the mountain rose up and appeared almost black in the wild tangle of barren salmonberry brambles and overgrown mossy rootwads. I could make out the pale fallen leaves of the devil's club. They were damp and matted against the mossy floor. There was one ancient alder tree that must have been four feet at the base, whose trunk went two hundred feet up and spread in silhouette against the steep wall of the mountain rising. Its major limbs arched up from the point where they split from the trunk, arched up severely in the gesture of a child being held forcefully by the wrists. The smaller limbs were a wild tangle of fingers that spread out and down toward the black mirror of the water. At the base of this tree I could see a vague shape of a straight line and then the intersection that formed a right angle. In the center I saw four ghostly white rectangles floating in an unnatural form. Then I saw the jagged straightness of steps and I recognized the cabin where Louis Victor had been murdered.

The mergansers eased past again, worked their way down the hull of the *Oso*, nudging along the waterline, then past the stern and out of sight. As I zipped up my pants, I could hear their squeaking exhalations and the wet beating of wings as they gained speed and flew.

I remembered Eli Hall, who murdered his girlfriend down in Craig. They had been drinking and he stabbed her in the chest. When he came to in the morning he loaded her body in a skiff and took it around the corner to one of his favorite crabbing spots and dumped it over the side. He knew it must have been two hundred feet deep. He slung her over the side and she sank about four feet below his skiff and then held there, neutrally buoyant. She was facedown, drifting as if on a meat hook, her gingham housedress moving slightly like a sea anemone caught in the light. When he reached with his oar and poked her, she rolled and the air escaped her lungs like a bellow and she sank in a swirling garland of bubbles and tentacles of light brown hair falling away. As he sat in jail he told me he didn't care how much time he got, he just wanted that picture of her sinking beneath his skiff out of his head.

Murder is about the death of memory. I had forgotten that, until I saw the little cabin in the tangle of the mountain. More than two years ago Louis Victor had lead driven through his skull and everything he knew spilt out of him into the ground and was lost. What I had investigated so far was the faint heat of that explosion, but here, now, I was at ground zero. I was in place, if not in time, and I had to dig the ground for whatever memory was left. All I had was my fuzzy senses, a man I at least half trusted, and the story of a woman who had married a bear.

SIXTEEN

IT WAS RAINING on the deck above my head when I awoke in the darkness. I could hear the drops running off the gunnels and into the water. I could hear the water breaking on the rocks. I felt the roll of the hull at anchor. I opened my eyes and saw Walt lighting the lantern in the first granite light of a wet October morning. I rolled back over and dug my feet down to find the warm pockets of air in the sleeping bag.

Walt hung the lantern above the narrow stairwell that led to the wheelhouse. Its light gave the cabin the sepia tone of an old photograph: oiled wood, shadows, and the incessant rain overhead. He started an alcohol stove and put a pot of fresh water on to boil. He set the old blue enameled pot on the stove and after a few seconds it began to rumble.

I took my jeans out of the bundle that I had used as a pillow, dragged them inside the sleeping bag, pulled them on over my legs, and wiggled around to button them up. They were dishearteningly damp and cool. As I stretched up to pull my socks off the rack above the oil stove I could see my breath in a damp spume of vapor.

Walt, who had not spoken yet, handed me a cup of tea even before I had my shirt buttoned. The tea was fragrant with oranges and I let the steam roll up into my eyes as I sucked up the first sip. Walt watched me and saw that I was ready to be spoken to.

"What do you think? What should we look for?"

"Well . . . I might just look around. I don't know . . . for anything . . . out by where they found the body. But you could see if you can find a place where he might have hidden a rifle. You think there might be a place like that in the cabin?"

"I would bet my life on it. He had little hidey-holes all over. Places that no one else ever knew about. When you escort drunken hunters, you take charge of their weapons at night. Louis knew about guns. He said they weren't any good to you if they were in the wrong hands. He always kept control of them. Always. That was the rule."

"So you go look for that and I'll look for anything else that might be around. But only after breakfast."

We ate oatmeal with raisins out of the same cups we had had our tea in. I put on my down vest and rubber boots and grabbed my wool cap and rain gear and stood by the ladder. Walt looked at me. He had his deer rifle slung over his shoulder. He held out a small .44-caliber five-shot revolver with a rounded hammer in a small leather holster.

"You want to carry this?"

"No."

"You want a drink?"

"No, I guess not."

He smiled at me as he pulled on his rubber raincoat and pocketed the revolver.

"You look a lot better to me today. Even so, I'd give you the whiskey or I'd give you the gun, but I sure as hell wouldn't give you both."

"Smart man."

"Yeah." He smiled. "Smart." He lifted the weight of the revolver in his pocket and his smile dimmed a little.

Above his trolling pit in the stern he had a platform slung between the posts for his gurdies. We hauled an aluminum skiff down off the platform and lowered it into the water. Then Walt unbolted a five-horse engine from the inside of the pit and handed it down to me in the skiff. After I screwed it to the transom of the skiff, he handed me the rest of the gear. The daypacks, the fuel tank, and the oars. I held on to the stern and steadied the skiff as Walt hung his legs over and climbed in. I pulled on the cord until the engine turned over once and then I reset the choke. The engine fired on the first pull. I sat down and steered toward shore.

The rain was gentle now, coming from heavy low clouds that showed their wet bellies to the water. We were in a long inlet on Admiralty Island. From our anchorage we could look out to the west to the main coast of Admiralty. Two peaks to the south showed through the overcast. The fresh snow on the upper slopes mixed with the light overcast near the sun and the gray of the rocky coastline mingled with the green gray of the water. I took in a deep breath and imagined the inside of my skull as a gray-green landscape, perfectly suited for this world.

Old-squaw ducks paddled on the surface, pushing forward, the hulls of their bodies gently rocking as they pushed, their eyes alert and their heads darting back and forth in a continual scan of the surface. To the south a quarter mile, some humpbacks were breaking the surface, and the ducks were making their way in that direction.

As we came into the shallows I lifted the engine and we eased into the shore, which was large cobbles of granite. Walt and I stepped out into the shallow water and pulled the skiff up onto some drift logs near the tide line. The tide was high and just beginning to go down. We could carry or drag the skiff back down to the water when we needed to go. Walt played out a bow line, tied the skiff to the trees, then squatted down and began fishing around in his pack. He found cartridges for his rifle and fed them into the magazine of his gun. He was quiet and there was an important sense of purpose to his acts. It was clear this was not a hunting jaunt or a mere work trip.

We had agreed he would inspect the cabin first. I would walk around the area, head out to the small estuary where the body had been dragged, and see what the country looked like. We didn't speak, but walked north up the stony beach. Walt turned up the path through the beach grass toward the cabin and I continued another fifty yards up the beach before cutting through the thick fringe of low alder trees.

Walking through the alders, I saw that the ground was matted with fallen leaves turned almond brown in the first stages of decay. They were slick and limber, beginning their seasonal compost. I pushed my way through the thinning limbs into an opening covered by a canopy of older trees. Here, the floor of the woods was a thick mattress of moss, dotted with ground-cover plants with heart-shaped leaves, and the walking was open. There were just a few scattered blueberry bushes, but they were bare. This fringe area was maybe twenty yards wide before the slope rose up steeply. On the slope the moss sloughed away slightly and rocks showed through. The spruce and hemlock trees were fat at the stump and did not seem to taper until high out of sight into the upper stories of limbs. It was quiet. I could hear the low-lying wheeze of the stream ahead of me and the light breathing of the saltwater back through the alder on my left.

I was following a narrow path that came from the cabin. The path was made by use, soft footing worn down through the moss. Here, where the skin of the forest floor was broken, I could look down to see the mass of roots and organic soil that lay like musculature under the covering of moss. The roots twisted and intertwined in one continuous fabric the entire length and width of the floor. You would be hard-pressed to single out one distinct plant from the whole growing mass.

Crows hopped in the blond stubble of beach grass and rocks to my left. They called and flew up in brief loops, taking mussel shells into the air and dropping them to try and force them open. I heard the continual chatter and clicks of their feeding as I walked into the forest. Periodically, I came across the dried broken shells of sea urchins and crabs. Otters had taken them from the tideflats up into the protection of the trees to eat. They left the shells on the moss like discarded toys.

The shelf narrowed as I approached the stream. The slope became a rocky bluff to my right, and I was left with a forty-foot path between it and the alders. I came across one ancient spruce tree that must have been twelve feet across at the butt. I stood next to it and looked up its length and all I could see was the thick limbs coming off the trunk several hundred feet above me. The trunk itself was twisted and gnarled and the bark was uneven. About eight feet up from the ground there were large gouges or wounds that showed black down into the sapwood and were weepy with pitch.

Large amber and white cakes of pitch ran toward the bottom
of the tree and claw marks raked down the bark. At the foot
of the tree I found the matted and strewn carcass of an
eagle: long hollow bones, thigh and shoulder. Intricate
curved architecture of the wing; the gray-green of feathers
and mold. Several large feathers from the wing. There was
no skull, no talons. I heard the first sizzle of wind several
hundred feet above me in the upper limbs of the ancient
tree.

I could sense no rain under the canopy, but as I pushed
out from it through the alders again I stepped into the
maritime weather. The rain was thick upon the estuary and
swirled like a young horse cantering around a corral. Much
of the tall grass had been laid flat by wind and heavy rain.
The tide was still high and the water was deep, moving up
the channel from the bay, becoming the channel of the
stream. The water swirled languidly with foam and spruce
needles forming gentle arches in the mud like crushed
shells on a coral beach thousands of miles away. I pulled my
hood up. The rain spattered down and the rings on the water
widened and crossed in confused patterns until all there
was was the drops bouncing back up through the surface
tension of the water as if they were trying to hop back up into
the sky.

To the west and out to the inlet the mud flat extended into
rocky tidelands. An immature eagle walked clumsily along
the mud and flattened eel grass. He waddled, muscular and
hunched, like a self-conscious young athlete. The crows had
given up their mussels and were pestering him, taking
short, swirling dives at his back and veering away. The eagle
plodded on toward a midden of clam shells and elephant-
colored rocks.

I walked along the edge of the meander, below the grass line and in the soft mud. I stepped into firm green bear scat wedged into the angular cut rocks near the water's edge. The salmon run in this stream was over but there were rotted corpses of pink salmon. Ugly, with hooked jaws and deformed backs. None had eyes in their sockets. Some swayed in the shallows of the brackish water, rotted white, with skeins of sloughed flesh twirling into the current, their mouths agape and grotesquely jutting to the surface. The air was thick with the smell of tide and pitch and dead fish in the soft mud.

I saw bear tracks in the mud, clear and finely etched. Claws perhaps four inches long coming from the toughened palm of the pad. They were headed in the direction I was going. I could see nothing ahead of me either on the bank or in the tall grass that ran down into the swampy flat of the river. I heard nothing. I cleared my throat and dug my hands deeper into my pockets and walked a little further upstream. I came to the narrowing point of the river where the freshwater stream fell through a short rocky falls into the tidal current. To my left was a dogleg cul-de-sac of grasslands and straight ahead was the steep slope of the mountain and heavy timber. I stopped, considering which way to go, when I heard a low grunt from a deep pair of lungs.

When I was young we lived in an old roadhouse in Juneau that had been a hunting lodge in territorial days. When my father came home from work it was almost of ceremonial significance. I would have the fire burning in the stone fireplace and my mother would have his drink ready. He sat in a leather chair and told us about his day, about the cases and the lives that had come before him. After about twenty minutes my mother would excuse herself and she would begin to set dinner on the table. Just after she excused herself, the Judge would turn to me and politely inquire about my day in school. I would give him some evasive and polite reply, and he would have a second drink. He understood I was evading him and he would move the subject to a hunting trip he planned to make, promising to take me on it. He talked about the duties of a man in the hunting camp and how a bear-hunting trip was no place for immaturity or silliness. When I was worthy I could go. He also talked about the bears on Admiralty Island and claimed they could touch the beams of our living room standing on their hind legs. I would look at him sitting in his leather chair, and above him the thick Douglas fir beams seemed unbelievably high. I thought the likelihood of my ever being old enough to go on such a hunting trip was slim. I watched him, tasted the smell of burning alder in the fireplace, heard the decorous clink of ice in his highball glass, and saw the bear standing behind him clawing the beams of our house. The presence of a bear that large was forever etched into my childhood imagination, and I had spent much of my adulthood trying to ignore it.

When the bear stood up in the tall grass beside the estuary in Prophet Cove, the dream world of my childhood house rose out of my body like cold sweat. The bear stood on her hind legs and I could see three-quarters of her torso. At first she did not move, and it was as if she were more a monument to a bear than an example of one. Then she swayed briefly like the top of a tree being felled. Her fur was matted down by the water she had been wallowing in and her coat was slick against her torso. She had the well-defined musculature of a middle-weight champion and the bulk of a Mercedes-Benz. As she stood there, water ran down her body and etched the pathways of the blood vessels and the knotted bundles of muscle, down the bulk of her shoulders and front legs, down her stomach past the visible row of teats that I could see just above the grass. She stood with apparent grace and power like Michelangelo's *David*.

Her head swayed, her tiny black marble eyes searched for me. Her coffin-shaped snout twitched and scanned, twitched and scanned. Her ears were erect. I heard the heavy bellows of her breathing and I tasted the scent of rotted fish and blueberry shit. I imagined her great warm bowels and the row of blunt teeth that would grind my bones to slurry. It was like staring into the sun: I had to avert my eyes and look down at the mud. I did not run, I did not say anything. I listened and waited.

Out of the corner of my eye I saw a woman walking along the beach fringe, one hundred feet to the right and toward the shore. She jumped over the bear scat and was gone into the woods.

The bear was down and running. Toward me. The snuffling grunts of breath broke through her teeth. Toward me. Running hard and outstretched like a thoroughbred, warm breath, slaver, the stench of rotten meat and tideflat, small, impassive eyes and the black rubbery rind inside her lips. Her teeth. The bulk of her body coming over me like a breaking wave.

I fell backward and she ran over me and up into the dense cover of the alder trees and into the forest. I heard the small trees snapping as she clawed up the steep rock slope, not slowing down or stumbling once. The clattering of rocks and the grunting up the hillside became more and more faint. I felt the icy hot needles of fear stabbing up through my body and I lay still on the ground, shaking and muttering.

My pants were ripped and my thigh was bruised and cut slightly where she had pushed off from my weight. The hard corner of the tape recorder in my pocket had dug into my hip and it was sore. My clothes had the stink of rotten fat where I had touched her. My skin seemed hot but my body was freezing and I could not stop shaking. I sat up. I flexed my fingers and felt them move easily in their sockets. I put my hands over my eyes and ran them down my face and felt the soft elasticity of my lips. I ran my hands down my neck and my chest and felt my pulse beating up along the entire surface of my torso. My ears rang with blood pumping through the vessels, the air seemed sparkling and the rain glittered like dust. I heard voices and a woman crying out in the woods . . . and then a shot.

I supposed that the sow was some distance away by now. I tried to think if her teats showed she had young cubs with her but I could not make my mind focus. I kept seeing eyes, teeth and black gums. I reached for an imaginary gun. I tasted bile and my head ached. I heard another shot.

I moved down the estuary and into the woods toward the cabin. I walked quickly, but did not run. I felt like I could have sprinted up the mountain after her, my step was so light, but I forced myself to pause and tried to pull myself down out of the heightened reality created by fear—back into my usual dream state. I was pulling, pulling on my breath to slow down as I made it to the clearing where the cabin came into sight.

I heard voices, men's and women's, loud and argumentative. I did not hear words but tones, meter—contradiction and interruption. As I stopped and cocked my head, I realized the voices blended with the sound of the squall and the wind in the alders. I saw the *Oso* riding the weather at anchor and I saw a floatplane tied to a small buoy that was around the bight from our anchorage. Out of sight from our vantage point until now. It was the same floatplane that had been tied to Emma Victor's dock. I stepped lightly on the moss, aware of every sound I might make now. I heard the noisy rustle of my rain pants scratching against my boots. Someone was arguing, maybe beseeching.

The cabin was only about twelve by sixteen, and it was made from brown plywood with an old metal roof. There was a lean-to on the mountain side made of visqueen rolled in a pole on the bottom. There was one window on the water side. The door appeared to be the heaviest part of the wall, and both panels were reinforced with heavy driftwood planks. It had a rusty brass knob.

Walt stood outside with his hands hanging down at his sides. He stood so still it seemed an effort.

Lance Victor was in back of him with an automatic pistol in his hand.

"Stop shooting that damn thing. Can't you see he isn't going to tell you anything?" Norma was at her brother's elbow, shifting from foot to foot. "I think he's alone. I ran out to the creek and I didn't see anyone."

I got down low and crawled the length of a fallen tree to

get closer. I peered around the end of the splintered stump, my head next to the moss. More words emerged.

"You might as well kill me, boy." Walt looked up at Lance almost with pity. "I'm not going to lift a finger to help you."

Emma Victor stood in the doorway above Walt. She wore a red mackinaw. She had her arms folded and stared at the back of his head. Lance pointed the pistol at Walt, the six-inch barrel wavering slightly.

"Don't tell him anything. We ask the questions," Emma said.

"But what if he won't talk, Mama?"

"Nobody cares anymore. Nobody except that foolish old woman, and I suppose that detective. Nobody cares about a killing when someone has already confessed."

"But what was he looking for here? Norma, do you know?"

Norma stepped up into the cabin and spoke so softly to her mother I could not hear.

"Well, look some more then. He must be snooping around for something. What was he doing under the bed, for God's sake?"

"Want to tell us now, Walt?" Lance waved the pistol under his nose like a piece of warm bread. "What were you looking for?"

"What are you going to do, boy? You going to push me into the bay? I might be harder to drown than De De."

Lance swelled inside his body and his hand trembled as he held the barrel of the gun tight to Walt's head. He began to speak in a shrill, pinched-off scream. "You're the one that was drunk that night, old man. You're the one that let her go up on deck. The weather was so bad. Why was she up on deck when we were moving the boat? What was she doing there? She saw too much. She saw too much because *you* were drunk. So I had to do what I did."

Norma came out of the door and held out her hand toward Walt. She could have been crying. "Walt, she saw Papa and Hawkes fighting. But she also saw Lance and me moving the boat. I didn't know what else she saw. I didn't know. Lance didn't know. When we heard that she was going to testify at the trial Lance went down to talk to her, to tell her to keep quiet if she knew anything more. I guess they got in a fight on the dock. She fell in by accident. It was an accident. Lance wouldn't deliberately kill her. It was an accident." Her voice trailed off.

Walt stared past Lance and his gun to Norma, standing on the steps. "You poor dumb kid. What makes a girl like you so simple and so mean?"

Norma shook her head and whispered "No" as she brushed the imaginary hair away from her forehead.

"It may have been an accident when she fell off the dock. But it sure as hell wasn't an accident when he pushed her back in the water. When he kicked her face and forced her underwater. That was no accident. I knew she was pregnant, I knew about her boyfriend and how he didn't want to be the father. I wanted to bring her home but I didn't. . . . Because he executed her."

Lance glanced at his sister and said in a soft voice, "Baby . . . I had to kill her. I had to. I told the police we slept all night. I couldn't let them question her again."

Then he jerked Walt's head back. He looked for his mother but she had stepped back into the cabin.

His cheeks were round and his skin was blotchy red like a sullen child's. He pulled back the hammer of the pistol and Norma buried her face in her hands.

I could hear Emma walking on the plywood floor inside the cabin.

"What were you searching for, Walt? What is there out here that could make any difference after all this time?" Lance asked once more.

"He was looking for this."

Emma stood in the doorway. She was holding a rifle. A bolt-action 45–70. On the stock near the trigger guard I could see three raking scratches where a bear had clawed. She pulled back the bolt and pushed a cartridge into the chamber. The bolt was very rusty, but she worked it forward and locked it down with a soft, substantial click.

"It's Louis's rifle. It was hidden under the floorboards, in a box. He was looking for this."

Lance sat down on a kindling splitting stump and rubbed the barrel of his pistol against his temple, muttering, "No, no, no."

"Lance!" Emma snapped from the doorway. "Lance, look at me." He swung his head around in her direction.

"Lance, why didn't you do something about this?"

Lance looked down at the wood chips as he spoke. "I didn't know where it was. I had to pump up the rubber boat we kept below before I could go ashore. The rifle was gone when I got to the beach. I checked all of the spots where I knew Dad hid things and it wasn't there. I never . . . I never figured it was still in the cabin. I thought that crazy fucker really had thrown it in the water. But I didn't know where. So I threw mine in the bay and told the cops where to find it."

"Well, it was. Too many people can identify this as his gun."

She looked at Walt as if from a distance. Then she stared down at the rifle and slowly nodded her head. She was weighing her choices, and I had a bad feeling about how things were tipping.

I stood up. I fumbled in my pocket. I cleared my throat but before I could give my assessment of the situation, Emma fired the rifle.

The bullet hit the bark of the spruce tree two feet from me. She was looking down the iron sights for a second shot. I raised my hands.

"Step down here, Mr. Younger." She motioned with the front sight.

I walked to the cabin and stood by the wall, my arms in the air.

"We should work something out," I whispered under my breath. I nodded at Lance.

Walt moved closer to me; we stood almost elbow to elbow. Lance could hold his gun on both of us now, so he was comfortable. Walt's hands eased into the pockets of his wool jacket.

"Emma, why? Why any of it?" he asked, looking up at her.

She did not pause and she did not waver in her answer. "He humiliated me. He humiliated his children. Then he wanted a divorce. A divorce. What would that leave me with?"

"He was killed to preserve the family?" I know I shouldn't have put it that way.

She almost smiled at me. She raised the rifle to her shoulder, but then lowered it and sat down on the steps.

"I'm a funny woman, Mr. Younger. I suppose after living with Louis for so many years I have a high tolerance for contradiction." I saw her fingers tighten around the grips of the 45–70. "But you're right. There was something more, even if it is hard for anyone else to understand."

She looked up at me and she narrowed her eyes. "I loved him . . . completely. We were one body and one flesh.

"This was a new world for me and I gave myself to it. Louis, Alaska, this life . . . everything was different. I smelled things I never had before. I saw things I could not have even imagined. I gave myself to that new life and to these children. How could I allow that to be taken away from me?"

Lance was standing, shifting his weight from side to side, fiddling with the gun. Norma looked at the ground.

"When I discovered that he loved someone else . . . I realized that there was part of him, maybe most of him, that was a stranger to me. He was someone I loved, but didn't know."

She cradled his rifle on her lap. "These are my children. It's true that they are half his. But I taught them to speak. I taught them to think and to love. They never really knew their father either. It was better to preserve at least some of his memory and his love than to let him desert them. Us."

She raised the front sight of the rifle and made figures in the air. "And these children are a damn sight better off with me than in prison."

Norma brushed her hand across her brow. Then she looked at me and squinted before she spoke.

"It wasn't Mama, Mr. Younger. I know what you're thinking. But you're wrong.

"Why did I shoot him? I don't think of it that way. I don't remember the gun or the moment before or after. I just see him fall.

"I loved my papa but I see him fall and something lifts up

inside of me, as if . . . as if I just thought of a word I couldn't remember. I feel lighter as I see him fall."

She turned and lifted the stick in front of her foot and tapped it lightly on the toe of her heavy leather boot. "When I was little, my papa took me berry picking. We would work down by the stream and he would tease me about stepping in bear shit. He would tease me and make grunting noises and he would scare me. I would cry and he would laugh. Laugh. He'd say that it was bad luck to step in bear shit. I told my friends in school it was bad luck for girls to step in bear shit, and they laughed, too.

"For a long time I thought they were laughing because it was funny. But then some of them started to call me names. They would laugh and pretend to be drunk and wave bottles at me and yell, 'Heap bad luck. Heap bad luck.' They'd act drunk and fall all over themselves laughing."

She looked up at me and now her eyes were watering as if the wind was blowing grit into them.

"By the time I was a teenager, I hated his being an Indian. I hated it in school. I hated it when boys would come over and their faces would change when they saw him in front of the TV and they realized where my dark hair came from. I hated it in airports when we traveled. He would walk into the clean, fancy terminals and if he stood in the wrong line people would talk to him too loud and slow. I hated the way he sounded, and I hated the way his hands felt when he had been drinking: soft and squishy, without a grip.

"I hated it . . . but . . . I loved picking berries with him. We would pick up Grandma and she would bring big pans that had come from the old cannery days. We carried them down by the river and she would hum slow tunes—bouncy tunes—chants, I guess, but I never knew the words. He would tear off branches and let me eat the ripe berries from them, as if they were lollipops. I liked that.

"When I was a freshman in high school I pretended that he wasn't my papa at all. He was a guide I had hired. More than a guide, a paid companion. He was devoted to me and he would tell me secrets and bring me treats when I wanted them. He was to be my companion until my real father came to claim me and take me off to San Francisco. I imagined waving from the deck of a steamship to this big Indian man standing in his rubber boots and canvas jacket as my real father wrapped me in a Hudson Bay blanket and led me into our stateroom. But that never happened.

"I loved Papa. I never planned to shoot him.

"I saw them from the bow of the boat. I saw them fighting. First I thought of protecting my papa. I thought of shooting Hawkes, but when I raised Lance's rifle and the sights lined up on Papa, something lifted up in me and—I pulled the trigger.

"I was ready to go to jail but Lance said he would take care of things. From there on in, we just did what had to be done."

Lance moved his head back and forth and narrowed his small eyes. His hand was bone white and tense around the grips of the gun. He looked sad, angry, and confused. A slow-witted man without his mother's tolerance for contradiction. A very dangerous man.

"But Todd?" I asked.

Emma lifted her rifle off her lap casually. "I was not . . . am not . . . going to let anything happen to my children. Your friend got between me and you. It was too bad. You started to stir things up and I didn't want that.

"I saw my mother-in-law that day. Then I took the gun, and gave a man's description to the police. That night I knocked on your door and waited. I thought you lived alone and I was thrown off by the half-wit. Then I thought you would be the next one out the door. I shot too soon. It was regrettable. It caused a lot of problems."

"Problems. Well, yes. But I still think we can work something out," I said. I looked at her carefully, searching for an angle.

"I think you're absolutely right, Mr. Younger." She lowered the rifle to her hip, apparently relaxed. And then she fired.

Walt rocked back and lay on the ground, sputtering. There was a tiny hole in his jacket just to the center of his breast pocket, but under his back a pool of blood spread into the mossy spruce needles and rotted alder leaves. He gasped, his hands still in his pockets, and then he lay still. The air was bitter with gunpowder. He looked undignified and forlorn, like a photograph of a victim from a cheap detective magazine.

"You two should not have interfered, Mr. Younger. You made too much noise."

I said his name. I bent over him and spoke into his ear. I reached inside his pocket and took the .44 in my hands.

I stood up and took Norma by the elbow and pressed the muzzle of the gun to her temple.

"This is very sloppy. I don't know what we are going to do." I backed toward the water with absolutely no idea of what my next step might be.

"But if you or Lance start shooting again I'm going to have to . . . I don't know . . . I guess . . . ," and I jammed the muzzle of the gun tighter against Norma's scalp.

Lance looked back and forth between me and his mother and then down at Walt, dead on the ground. The pistol was still tight in Lance's grip.

Norma's body was rigid and she breathed in shallow gasps. I walked us backward awkwardly over the slick cobbles.

Emma stepped down and came toward her daughter and me. "I think you're right. I'm sure we can work this out. Lance and I will get in the plane. We will fly to the beach just on the other side of the ridge. Let Norma go. She can hike over and meet us. We'll say Mr. Robbins killed himself out of grief for his daughter. We'll leave it at that. Now we'll go to our plane, Mr. Younger.

She nodded to Lance and he moved toward a small inflatable kayak lying inside Walt's tin skiff. I hadn't agreed to the plan but it was being carried out. Lance launched the kayak and they both got in. With the two of them in it, the kayak looked foolishly small, like a bathtub toy. Lance paddled them out to the plane about fifty yards from shore. Once there, he handed their packs up to his mother and then the rifles.

Norma and I stood on the beach. I dropped my right hand holding the .44 to my side. She was sobbing.

They let some air out of the kayak and wedged it into the backseat of the plane. Emma got into the pilot's seat and Lance balanced on the struts under the propeller to reach the passenger side. Once in, he reached behind his seat. The engine turned over and the propeller spun. Emma opened her door and yelled to Norma above the propwash, "Just walk to the beach across the point." She turned the plane north, into the wind.

Lance raised the rifle to his shoulder. Norma screamed and ducked. I didn't hear anything but the slug bit my left arm and spun me around to my knees.

Norma ran.

I braced myself on one knee and tried to steady the pistol. I fired twice into the cowling around the airplane motor. I saw nothing. The engine's whine did not change pitch. Emma swung the plane away from the beach and gave it full throttle. It lumbered across the water and finally lifted into the air, water trailing from the floats.

The silence eased around us. Norma stood at the water-line. She watched the plane, shifting from foot to foot like a bowler doing a little body-English dance. She was crying as she watched. The plane, now three hundred feet off the water, banked to the west. It circled around as if to land again, and as it passed I saw oil streaking down the cowling, then black smoke. The engine sputtered. As a gust of wind came from the head of the inlet the plane tumbled, cart-wheeling in the air like a toy.

Norma stood still, not making a sound, as she watched the plane slide and flail its way into the water. But when the fuselage of the aircraft broke away from the floats and sank, she buried her face in her hands.

The plane's supports bobbed up. A few moments later I saw two figures clamber up and cling to the aluminum floats. They hauled themselves clear of the water and leaned against the wrecked undercarriage.

There was aluminum debris and oil floating on the surface.

Some old-squaw ducks paddled nearby and the whales were feeding complacently a quarter of a mile to the south.

Toddy was probably hooked up to some machine in the hospital and somewhere up the hill I imagined the bear was scratching at the roots of a skunk cabbage plant. And Walt was dead.

I sat on a rock, threw the gun down at my feet, and tried not to think about these things all at once.

SEVENTEEN

TODDY'S HOSPITAL BEDSIDE table looked like the shrine of Fatima. Every good Christian in town had taken the opportunity to try to win his simple heart for the Lord. I sat next to his bed in an armchair. The TV was on, but I had turned the radio off. Todd was playing some kind of electronic baseball game, holding it in his hands and bumping his thumbs around on buttons. He had four cans of juice on his table and a bucket of ice. Sitting on an extra TV stand was his fish tank. The killifish bumped against the glass and under the arches of a plastic castle. The fish tank had a large and stately presence in the room, like a national park.

"Cecil, are they going to arrest you for killing Mr. Robbins?" He did not look up.

"I told you. The police said they wanted to investigate thoroughly and they might take it to the grand jury, but they just didn't know. They're still going over the scene. Emma and the 'kids' went out to the house in Tee Harbor to wait."

"Didn't you tell the police what really happened?"

I strained in my chair and thought about asking him to

put down the game if he wanted to talk about my participation in a killing. But I didn't.

"Yes, I told them what happened. I went out to the *Oso* and used the radio to call the Coast Guard and the troopers. They came out by helicopter and fished Emma and Lance out of the water. I gave a statement that night, and the troopers patched up my arm."

"Did Emma tell them what happened?"

"Well, Todd, I think she did. But I think she told them that I killed Walt and then tried to murder her family."

"Doesn't that worry you?"

"Yeah, a little. But I gave them the rifle and that should help. And I also have some insurance."

"Insurance?"

"You know how sometimes I run my tape recorder without telling people?"

"I know." And here he looked up from his game. "That's not really fair is it, Cecil?"

"Well, it's not illegal. And I made a pretty good tape of the whole scene down by the cabin."

"Did you give it to the police?"

"Not yet. I want Emma to commit to her story. I want her to swear under oath and tell the world that she is absolutely sure that I threatened to shoot Walt unless he paid me to keep quiet about his murdering Louis. I want her to be frank and believable with an angelic look on her face—and then I'll give them the tape. But I'm going to wait and see. I'm going to give them the tape sometime. I just don't know when."

Toddy put his game down on the bed in the valley between his knees. He was tired and had been awake longer than he should have been. I had my jacket off and he looked at my arm where it was bandaged. He looked worried now, and his eyebrows knitted together in a long-held thought. He propped his glasses up off the bridge of his nose.

"There sure has been a lot of shooting."

"Yeah."

"And a lot of people killed. Why do you think that is, Cecil? I mean, we didn't do anything to anybody, did we?" Toddy doesn't cry when he is unhappy but he clenches his fists and starts to hyperventilate. He knotted his sheet in his fists.

"What's wrong, buddy? Do you need something?" I almost rang for the nurse.

"Cecil. One of those ladies who came and brought me these books about the Bible and all of this stuff . . . you know? Well, she said that I got shot because God knew that I was a strong person. She said that I got shot because God loved me and was giving me a test that he knew I was strong enough to pass."

He took his glasses off and looked at me with the dim sniffing gaze of someone who can't see a thing without his glasses.

"That seems crazy to me, Cecil."

"Me too, buddy." I leaned over and cradled his bristly head in my arms and hugged him. "That's crazy," I whispered.

"I immediately thought that, when she said that stuff." He leaned back and put his glasses on and smiled up at me with a bobbing, red-faced grin.

I leaned over his table and looked at some of the gifts on his bedside shrine.

"Speaking of good things. Did Hannah send you this?"

I picked up a jar of jam. I looked at the label taped on top of the gold lid. It read: "For Toddy—Salmonberry jam, Sitka. Picked by Hannah Elder and C. W. Younger/ 'By sweetness alone it survives.'"

On my way to the hospital I had stopped by the bench in front of the home and the book was there. Someone had wrapped it in plastic, knowing it would be missed. The cover was limber with moisture, the paper almost pulp again. I had it tucked in my pocket next to my tape recorder.

"She said when I got out of the hospital she was coming to visit."

"She did? You think I could have a taste?"

I started to twist off the lid, and then stopped to hear what he would say.

"Okay . . . I guess."

He was smiling but his eyebrows were twitching and I knew he wanted the first taste. I dug around on his lunch tray, then spooned up as much as I could balance on a little plastic spoon and held it to his lips.

"Thank you," he said and swallowed, then closed his eyes in a reverential grin of appreciation. "Ummmmm."

I smelled it first as if it were an old bottle of wine. I thought of the warm, bitter taste in my mouth as Hannah and I had walked back from the graveyard. I thought of that summer and how far off it seemed, how long the winter would be. But then I tasted how sweet the berries were.

"Are you crying?" Todd looked up at me with that quizzical expression of a dog watching you undress. "Cecil?"

"It's just very good jam, buddy. It's nice to taste it."

Todd was still a little feverish. He lay back in his bed and I cranked the head of it down and turned off the light. "I'll be back tonight," I said.

I eased my jacket on over my sore arm and walked out the

door of the hospital. I had to go down to the home and give
Mrs. Victor my final report. She already knew the facts. I'd
spoken to her over the phone and she'd thanked me and
asked me to help her find a good attorney for her grandchildren if they were going to have to stand trial. I thought
that was funny, seeing as how it was her grandchild who
pulled the trigger on her son. She said she understood that
but she still wanted to help. She said it was never about
blame, it was about making things right. She was a Christian
and she knew about making the world right . . . but she still
needed a lawyer. I told her to call Dickie Stein.

I asked Mrs. Victor over the phone how she knew that I
was telling the truth and she told me that it just made sense.
The police reports didn't make sense, but my story did.

We didn't mention the woman who had married a bear,
and I didn't ask her if it was a true story. I didn't even ask her
if she had just told it that way to ease me along the path of her
own suspicions. I kept my peace. Most old stories don't have
anything to do with facts; they're the box that all the facts
came in.

It was an early snow for October and I knew it would turn
to rain. My feet got soaked as I walked toward the cathedral.
A raven circled from over the landfill and flapped the dense,
snowy air above me. He landed on the stop sign in the main
intersection in town. He had a red thread wrapped around
his foot. Apparently, there was a kid who was desperate to
trap a raven and was not going to be dissuaded.

I knew that the cathedral was locked and no one was
there, but I also knew if I gave ten bucks to the right person
after the bars closed, I could get in and stay there until they
threw me out in the morning.